MYSTERY MEN
(& WOMEN)
VOLUME SEVEN

AIRSHIP 27 PRODUCTIONS

Mystery Men (& Women) Volume Seven

"A Walk in the Park: A Tale of the Exceptionals" ©2021 Teel James Glenn
"Rise of the Bund: A Kiri Adventure" ©2021 Curtis Fernlund
"Pimpin' Your Supercar: A Dr. Fixit Tale" ©2021 Greg Hatcher
"The Ghoul Strikes!" ©2021 Harding McFadden and Eleanor Hawkins

An Airship 27 Production
www.airship27.com
www.airship27hangar.com

Cover illustration ©2021 Adam Shaw
Interior illustrations ©2021 Rob Davis

Editor: Ron Fortier
Associate Editor: Gordon Dymowski
Marketing and promotion: Michael Vance
Production designer Rob Davis.

ISBN: 978-1-953589-12-5

Printed in the United States of America

10 9 8 7 6 5 4 3 2 1

MYSTERY MEN
(& WOMEN) VOLUME 7
—TABLE OF CONTENTS—

A WALK IN THE PARK
A TALE OF THE EXCEPTIONALS

By Teel James Glenn

Prologue:

It was not a world anyone wanted to live in except the terrorists. Their desperation to make the rest of the world conform to their view of the universe, as far back as the 1980s, had changed the world. It was a slow change at first, and then after the horrors that followed until finally the stadium massacre of 2025 was like a dam that burst; the violence and irrationality of their vision was imposed on the rest of the world.

It was from the chaos and lawlessness that a terrified world came to embrace the concept of The Exceptionals, modeled after the 1871 bounty hunting law in the United States: extraterritorial bio-enhanced bounty hunters, who could go anywhere, do almost anything in the name of justice and the law.

The United Nations mandated that their identities become a closely-guarded secret.

Chosen by governments from existing elite law enforcement and military operatives they all had lives, some dark and some in the light, before they put on the mantle of service. They left those identities behind to live in the glare of the public eye; marked men and women who lived a day at a time.

◉◉◉

Conner Le'Schott, whom the world knew by his Exceptional codename Lastshot, picked up the trail of the Lithuanian Aurilis at *Le Park*. Lastshot had been looking for the arms dealer for weeks through the back alleys of Europe and had all but given up any hope of finding him. He was the last link to a case in the mountains of Panama where stolen nuclear triggers had been made available to the black market. Aurilis had purchased those triggers and the governments of the world and Unipol wanted them back.

Le Park was in a section of Paris, France that used to be pleasant apartment buildings. It was East of the *Ill Saint Germain* in the *Issy Les Moulineaux* area. After the Food riots of twenty twenty-three and the Second Muslim War it was no longer a pleasant area.

The *Park Suzanne Langlen,* the real name of the area at the north of the section, had become a squatter's camp after the war and stayed one in the chaos that followed. It became one of the enclaves outside the all-seeing

6

eyes of the observation cameras that had become standard in all the major cities in the twenty first century. It was a no-man's land where the conventional French Provincial Police dared not venture except in force.

Ultimately *Le Park* ended up becoming a black market bazaar where most things off the European Union's legal list could be obtained with no questions asked for the right number of untraceable credits. That included suppressed nano-tech, bio-sludge and armaments of every description. Unipol suspected the nuclear triggers had passed through the market less than a month before.

Le Park was a maze of tents and a chaos of color and style. The plastic and plastisteel stalls bore more than a passing resemblance to an Arab bazaar. Little of the green park that the market had grown over was left save for the few hardy trees that still poked through the rabbit warren of sellers.

French, Arabic, German, English and several dialects of Chinese all added to the Babel-like sound of the market, a constant buzz of arguments, bargaining and bartering. 'Jackers, hackers and cyber traders were everywhere. The air of the park was a heady mix of smells; humanity packed too tightly, refuse not cleaned away, sewage runoff and multiple cooking stalls of a world of cuisine.

Peppered in among the dealers in wares were the sex providers who couldn't get a work card for the *Vanes* district. Thus an inner economy within the outlaw economy flourished with the providers, male and female often trading for the drugs Boost or Stim—the two newest ways to forget the world that required them.

Lastshot was dressed in civies, with a long grey leather trench over his leather Exceptional's Battle Dress suit in blue and red, but was still an impressive sight at a muscular two meters tall. His long salt and pepper hair was cut in a retro mullet style and did little to conceal his square jawed rugged good looks.

He wore what looked like conventional dark sunglasses but were, in fact, neural glasses that were jacked directly into his mind through contact points on his temples and allowed him to see in several ranges; infrared, ultraviolet and thermal imaging. He used those functions to keep Aurilis in sight as the squirrelly blonde moved through the narrow pathways of the market.

"Lastshot to Blue Dove on a comcheck, over," he whispered into a comlink at his lapel. He spoke with a soft southern drawl.

"Blue Dove listening, *Monsieur Le'John Wayne*." A sweet female voice came through the earjack on his glasses. "I can hear you loud and clearly. Can you still see the Lithuanian? Over."

Lastshot laughed at the French Exceptional's way of referring to him. She was all of a meter and a half tall, with dyed blue hair and a coquettish smile. They had been working on the case for over two weeks together and she delighted in taunting him about being very American. She was also one of the best agents that Unipol had so he had come to expect and even enjoy her taunts.

"The little rat is haggling over a shipment of cutrate landmines to sell to the Tibetan Liberation Front." Lastshot said, "He is not only an evil Son-of-a-Bitch but tighter with a euro than my grandmother's corset! Over."

"You Americans talk so funny," she said. "How do you get anything done with such an ugly language? Over."

This made him laugh out loud and he had to stifle it for fear of drawing attention to himself. He was standing in the shadow of a needle gun seller's booth, pretending to look over the deadly inventory. He was trying to show just enough interest to not be shooed away and not so much interest that the booth's owner would monopolize his time. All the while he was watching Aurilis who was four booths away.

Lastshot did his best to listen with a tiny directional microphone hidden in a ring that had been programmed to filter all voices and sounds but the Lithuanian's and those directly near him.

I will take delivery at the Blue Eyed Horse," the Lithuanian said to the booth dealer he was talking with. "The credits go you your Cayman Account when I see the shipping statements."

"Of Course," the stall dealer said in Farsi, "and the detonators will follow the credit transfer?"

"Absolutely,"Aurilis said, "it's all a matter of verifiable trust—"

As he watched Lastshot saw two other figures move up to his prey and he heard the arms dealer scream "*Damn Mickey!*" and take off at a dead run.

"He's on the move, fast!" Lastshot said. "Somebody else is chasing him!" The long-legged Exceptional dropped all pretense and headed off into the crowd toward his quarry at a quick walk.

"Move in, move in!" Lastshot dodged and ran through the crowd like a broken field football player. His long coat flowed behind him like a cape.

Ahead he could see the three figures also running at a full clip with considerably less skill than his own. Even if he didn't have the thermal imaging function he could have followed their progress by the multi-lingual curses that erupted to mark their path.

"Red," Lastshot called out, "they are heading your way toward the tracks; remember we want Aurilis in a talkative mood."

"I'm on it, Big Wolf!" A new female voice came through his com-link. "I guess I need the aerobics. Over."

Lastshot smiled. He knew that his American teammate, codenamed Skorpion, hated to run; she was a full-figured woman and though in great shape she favored shooting running suspects in the legs rather than chasing after and tackling them. "Conservation of energy" she called it.

Knowing that his redheaded comrade was ahead by the commuter train tracks, Lastshot veered away from the trio ahead and made a run toward *Av Emile Zola* to try and outflank his quarry.

His stride was easy and long-legged as he moved to the edge of the market. He made better time on the fringe streets than in the center of the crowd. When he rounded a booth he got a clear look at the runners ahead of him.

Aurilis was almost as tall as the American Exceptional though more lanky. He had a pinched face and haunted blue eyes beneath thinning blonde hair. The two chasing him were as odd a pair as Lastshot had ever seen.

The runner in the rear was a bear of a man with a graying beard and an automatic pistol in his right hand. He raised it to fire a shot past his own companion and took a quick shot at the Lithuanian that missed by a few feet.

The lead runner with the bearded man was shorter than his companion by a head and was all lithe muscle that showed even through his tailored suit. When the shot missed Aurilis he waved the gunman off and put on a burst of speed to overtake their rabbiting victim.

Lastshot did a thermal scan of the younger pursuer and could see he was not carrying a gun but had a Bowie knife in a waist sheath and two slender knives up his sleeves for throwing. He radioed those facts to his two teammates.

"I will take ze Lithuanian," Blue Dove said in her soft lilting accent. "I can see him now."

"I got Santa Claus," Skorpion said. "You get the pacifist who doesn't like bang sticks."

"You are so generous, Red," Lastshot said, just a little out of breath from the run. "So you can buy dinner later; but no snails. I hate snails."

⊙⊙⊙

Skorpion was an impressive woman. Even without her normal Exceptional battledress uniform in hues of scarlet she had a presence that dominated any room she was in—when she wanted to. She could also all but disappear in a crowd when she wanted to and that is what she was doing while providing rear guard security on her partner Lastshot at the edge of *Le Park*.

She wore a hooded leather trenchcoat over her BDU to conceal her red hair and the blue tattoo of a scorpion that crawled down from its curled stinger above her left eye to left cheek.

She hid in plain sight standing at one of the electronic stalls conversing in Hindi with the seller, discussing a rebuild on a satellite intercept monitor. He made no secret of his admiration of her full figure and muscular legs barely contained in her combat pants. She smiled knowingly at him and drove a hard bargain for the components.

While she haggled she listened to her earwig comlink and kept her eyes scanning the bazaar around her.

She sipped a bottled vitamin water and was thinking about getting some goat on a stick from the booth next to the dealer, one of her favorite treats, when she saw a burnoose-wearing man several booths down a row to her left. Her attention was drawn to him by a song he was humming as he walked past. It was an old Kurdish Shepard tune she knew well.

"Of Treasures many my quests have found
Adventure and danger as well,
But of certain nothing like the loss of love
Is a surer passage to hell…"

Suddenly Lastshot's voice came over the earwig comlink. "He's on the move!"

◉◉◉

Vilna Aurilis was a man who lived his life on the edge, always looking over his shoulder for the last person he had swindled to be trying to even the score. So he wasn't surprised when he saw Vladimir Yolinko approaching him with an underling in Le Park. He had, after all, cheated "Mickey" Michencko on a shipment of rail-gun parts but he never expected the Russian would send his bullyboy into the heart of Europe for such a small matter, a few hundred million credits.

And he expected perhaps a beating or long lecture and a few broken fingers, but when he saw Vladimir reaching for his pistol and the look in the big Russian thug's eyes he knew that Mickey had decided to make an example of him and chose the better part of valor.

He knew that if he could make it deeper into *Issey Les Moulineaux* he would be able to lose the killers and then use his contacts to smuggle himself out to his hideaway outside of Rio De Janeiro.

"Damn Yolinko, the big animal!" he thought as he raced through the stalls of the market. "He is faster than he looks." And the little one with him was worse.

Aurilis thought he might make it as he cleared the last booth and headed across the tracks of the commuter local train when the Yolinko took a shot at him.

The Lithuanian knew he had nothing but open ground before him for a thousand meters until he could make it to the rundown apartment buildings where he could hide, and he had no chance of avoiding a second shot.

He started to turn to try to talk his way out of a headshot when a red fury seemed to explode from a side alley and slammed into the bearded man's pumping legs, bowling Yolinko over so that the two went rolling across the pavement and the gun went flying.

A tall, trench-coated man also had joined the chase and jumped clear of the two tangled bodies with a long-legged leap.

Aurilis' more immediate concern was Yolinko's companion who was also in the chase, a man he knew as *Carouche*. He was the one the locals called "The Slitter" because he never used a gun.

Aurilis wasted no more time in any attempt to talk. He turned and raced for the apartments again.

"I can beat him," he thought. "He can't throw and run."

So the Lithuanian smuggler applied himself to gaining more speed over the rough gravel of the rail bed.

◎◎◎

Skorpion slammed into the running Russian thug with her best football tackle, taking the three-hundred pound criminal down with a bone-jarring, rolling impact. She liked a rough and tumble fight and she knew when she hit him that she was in for one.

Yolinko slammed into the pavement at the edge of the gravel trackbed with no idea who had attacked him or why. He rolled over as the female Exceptional rammed into him, causing him to lose his gun on impact.

"I am a registered Exceptional," she yelled as she rolled with him. "I am ordering you to surrender."

Yolinko's response was to drive his elbow down on the head of the woman to clear her off him. She hunched her shoulders against the attack and caught the blow harmlessly on her trapezoid muscles.

He rolled clear.

The woman came to her feet as the Russian reared up. She saw the tell-tale sign that he was activating implants when his pupils enlarged and his face flushed. She guessed he had given a mental command to old military implants still in his system from his service time. He was clearly flooding his system with meta-amphetamines. It meant his strength and stamina would jump by a factor of three or more.

She would have a harder time bringing him down without shooting him. It made her wish she had brought her steel whip; it would have been a nice, quick way to end the fight with non-lethal results. It allowed her to use her "little secret"—her bio electric ability—without people realizing it was her and not the whip.

Yolinko roared a challenge and charged the woman who had dared assault him. His charge presented Skorpion with an answer to her problem.

She smiled with a cold joy at the challenge and accepted his charge with a cross-armed ju jitsu grab, pivoting her body to use his own momentum against him. Her hip throw sent him arcing high and wide, slamming hard into the rough gravel of the trackbed.

He felt no pain from the toss, rolling to his feet immediately and charging in again intent on overwhelming her. It was obviously how he always fought, roaring into an opponent like a Russian winter.

This time the Exceptional dropped back in a *tomanage*, a sacrifice throw. She placed one foot on Yolinko's chest as she grabbed his outstretched arms and dropped backward to the ground. As her back hit the ground she straightened her bent leg and propelled the big man over her with all the force she could muster.

She kept hold of his arms so he smashed into the ground with bone-jarring impact. It drove the air from his lungs and dislocated his left shoulder but with the drugs in his system he hardly felt it.

Yolinko reared up again and tried to swing a club-like fist at the woman's head but she had rolled up to her feet with the nimbleness of a woman half her size. She leapt into a spinning kick that slammed her booted foot into his right temple. The Russian dropped to the ground, unconscious, without a sound.

◉◉◉

Lastshot overtook the knife-wielding runner just before the man crossed the train tracks. He either sensed the Exceptional was on his heels or more likely heard his footfalls for as the American came abreast of him he suddenly stopped and slashed out at throat height with the Bowie knife from his belt sheath.

Lastshot detected the tension in the man's shoulders as he drew the blade. The lawman managed to duck the swing but kept moving forward. He turned to face the man.

"I am an Exceptional trying to arrest the man you are chasing," Lastshot said in French. "Back off and I will press no charges against you."

The knife man showed no inclination to comply.

Close up the man was clearly of Romany blood, with long dark hair, vaguely almond-shaped eyes and high cheekbones. His eyes were a startling green and cold with the calculating intensity of a born killer.

He showed neither joy nor fear as he advanced on the Exceptional. He shielded his knife with his off hand in the relaxed, natural crouch of a professional.

Lastshot would have preferred to just drill the guy in the head and continue on after the Lithuanian but he knew there would be all sorts of hell to pay with the French officials if he did. *"This really was so much simpler when I was doing black ops with a get-out-of-jail-free card. Dove will get the scumbag,"* he thought, *"I just have to keep laughing boy here from making me into a pincushion."*

The knifeman showed no inclination to rush into a fight. His breathing was even and his eyes focused.

Lastshot did a quick scan of his vital signs using the thermal function of his glasses and it showed the man was almost abnormally relaxed.

The American pulled off his coat and flung it aside, leaving him attired in his red and blue shortsleve uniform shirt. He hoped bare arms would be a tempting target for the knife.

Lastshot pumped adrenaline into his system at the same time stabilizing his heart rate. He also willed his neural glasses to send a real time image to a satellite uplink that would allow a record of the whole fight. It would make talking to a French judge after the fact less of a hassle.

The knifeman did not take the bait, instead adjusting his tactics when he realized that the Exceptional was not going to charge in blindly.

The Slitter moved forward to test Lastshot's reactions but did not actually attack. He had a completely poker face but his eyes missed nothing. Lastshot could tell the man was aware of all his slight movements, every adjustment of weight and slight twitch that the American made.

"Waiting for me to make a mistake," Lastshot thought. The two moved in

a slow widdershins circle, each a perfect mirror of the other's movements. *"Okay, I'm ready to screw up."*

The American started to step right and then shifted his weight slightly in a halting fashion as if he had changed his mind. He noted that the knife-man almost moved in at the hesitation but had the restraint to wait for a larger mistake.

Lastshot realized that the man was a very skilled knife fighter and would need more than a slight hesitation to risk committing to an attack against a larger and skilled opponent. He baited his "trap" to sweeten the enticement. He willed his glands to sweat and let his own calm expression slip slightly toward worried.

The knifeman moved in slightly to let the gap between them tighten.

Lastshot then stepped back with his right foot, giving ground with the ghost of fear in his attitude. This time the Romany took the bait and stepped in to slash at the exposed left side of the American.

Lastshot dropped into a crouch and spun his right foot in a scything leg sweep that took both legs out from under the knifeman. Before the knife-man hit the ground he threw the Bowie at the Exceptional's head in a move that would have been fatal if it had connected.

Instead of dodging the American speeded his reflexes up and caught the knife in midair by the handle.

By the time the Romany actually hit the ground he had both his throwing knives in his hands but he also had Lastshot's boot on his chest and the American's smart pistol pointed between his eyes.

"Go ahead and throw them. We'll see which is faster."

The knifeman showed no emotion as he dropped both knives and held his hands up, professional to the end.

◎◎◎

Vilna Aurilis made the shadows at the edge of the housing project on the opposite side of the tracks from *Le Park*. He paused, leaning against a crumbling wall to catch his breath. He could see the tall man in the grey trench coat clearly as he faced the Slitter. It brought a smile to his face.

"Perhaps they will all kill each other," he thought, "and I can have a quiet day."

"Please do not move," a soft female voice said from behind him. "I am the force of the law; you are under arrest for arms dealing."

Aurilis snapped his head around to see a vision in a tight-fitting blue leather jumpsuit. She had a short cloak cut with scalloped edges to evoke the image of wings.

"Le Blue Dove?" Aurilis said. He was struck by how bright her blue eyes were behind her domino mask. Her pretty features were firmly set and there was no softness when she spoke.

"I know my name, Monsieur Aurilis, as well as yours." The petite Exceptional said, "Please present your hands for cuffing."

The Lithuanian stood up straight and raised his hands with open palms. He smiled his best disarming smile and said, "I can imagine no greater delight, my dear Exceptional than to be restrained by you, though I wish it were not here in an alley."

◉◉◉

Lastshot triggered his com as soon as he had the knifeman on his face with his hand cuffed behind him. "Hey Red," he said, "how's things with Santa?"

"Wrapped for Christmas," she said. "I'm on my way to you, Over."

"Okay, that leaves you Madame Miniature," he said. He holstered his gun as he caught sight of Skorpion walking a very subdued Yolinko toward him.

There was silence on the com-link.

"Blue Dove," he repeated, "Do you read me? Over."

The silence became ominous when it persisted. "Dove?" he repeated with the tension evident in his voice. He listened so hard the silence was replaced by the beating of his own heart in his ears.

"Red, stay with these skells," he called to Skorpion. "I'm going after Dove!" He made sure that the Romany was clearly in sight of the redheaded Exceptional then commanded his glasses to call up the GPS transponder for the missing agent. When he had the transponder signal overlayed over a real time map of the area he ran for it.

He didn't have to go far.

The body of the French agent was lying behind a pile of broken packing crates in an alley just inside the perimeter of the housing project; face down with a throwing spike in the back of her neck at the base of her skull. The blood that had seeped from the wound stained the blue of her wig a muddy brown.

His scan of the body showed there was nothing but residual electrical activity in the brain; no blood flow, no sign of life at all.

Lastshot knelt down beside her and did his best not to show the rage he

"I can imagine no greater delight, my dear, than to be restrained by you..."

felt. He bit his lip hard enough to draw blood.

He gently touched the cooling flesh of her cheek with two fingers to say goodbye.

"I'll find him for you, Giulie," he said using the real name of the dead woman. Then he looked up at the dark shapes of the houses.

"No matter where you go, Aurilis," he whispered, "I will find you and when I do, I'm gonna gut you like the animal you are."

◎◎◎

"You can't go into the Blue Eyed Horse, Conner," Skorpion said to her teammate. "Aside from the fact that the French won't let you go on your own into that cesspool, you'll be made in a minute and dead in two." The two of them were sitting in the Paris offices of the Europack, the Exceptional group for the European Union.

They were dressed in their full public battle dress uniforms: He was in midnight blue and red leathers that, trimmed with white, gave him the aspect of a motorcycle thrill show costume. The red boots, with tooled eagles carved into them, and the neck scarf added just a touch of a movie cowboy. On his right hip in a tooled leather holster that added to the cowboy image was a smart carbine, keyed to his thoughts that allowed him to fire a range of ammunition by just willing it.

She wore shades of red, deep red loose pants and wide-sleeved shirt, soft desert boots and a deep red leather bustier that barely contained her ample bosom. Over it all she wore a long leather sleeveless robe that was incised with ancient Egyptian symbols that she had never explained to any of her colleagues. They were all too professional to ask why they were there. On her hip was her steel whip coiled and waiting for use and a nine-millimeter automatic.

The two had just come from a public ceremony to honor the fallen Exceptional that had been hastily organized by the French Government and a smaller, private ceremony held by her teammates.

Blue Dove's fellow Europack members had taken their friend's death with a Gaelic philosophical detachment that spoke to how deeply they felt for her. Several representatives of Exceptional teams from around the world had come as they were able to free themselves from other duties. The wake had been almost immediate because Blue Dove was Jewish and custom dictated it.

Some had been able to make the ceremony in person: Longbow, The

Highlander, Gael Force, and Silverarm of the United Union's Round Table; Nubia and Hyena of The African Union's Royal Lions; and Ajax of Greece's Titans. Other teams had sent Tri V tributes out of respect for their fallen comrade.

There had been a somber ceremony alone, in a temple near Notre Dame after the Tri V cameras had left and a bottle of wine was cracked on her behalf. Conner had been grim throughout; now, sitting with Skorpion and their Scottish comrade Highlander, he was seething with desire for vengeance.

"All I need is a minute with that dirtbag," the tall American said. "Then I don't really care; she didn't deserve to die."

The redheaded woman looked at him over the rim of a shot glass of Glenfinich Whiskey and narrowed her eyes with anger. "Don't give me that bullshit. You know she accepted the risks; we're lawmen, the chance of buying the farm is part of the cost of doing business." She drained the glass in one shot. "You of all people should be intimately aware of that fact."

He shot her an annoyed look and went back to staring out the window. "I can't believe they released the big guy and the Gypsy knifeman."

"What did you want? They said they were just "trying to collect a debt' from Aurilis. That Yolinko had a permit for his gun and there were no outstandings on them; we do have to uphold some laws, you know—we are technically cops."

Lastshot stood by the window staring out at the Eiffel Tower across the Champ-de-Mars. Created using the nonlinear integral differential equation to make it immune to wind damage, it was a marvel of science in its time. The nightlights on it didn't reveal the designated laser cage that protected it from another attack like the twenty twenty-three assault. Now, the first three hundred feet of the more than one thousand were encased in clear plexisteel. Once the peak of man's achievement and a pointer to the future, it had become a relic.

Lastshot realized that he was a relic in many ways, a man who had very old ideas of justice and vengeance; it was why he had become an Exceptional, because he believed that action rather than reflection was the way to solve problems. Because he believed in higher, older laws than man's that dictated an active participation in life.

And he was going to follow those "older laws" to find a way to make Aurilis pay for the little girl named Giulie St. Lurac who the world knew as The Blue Dove.

"Have you come to your senses about the Horse?" she asked. "There'll be another time for Aurilis." She refilled her glass and held the bottle poised over a second glass for him.

Jeremy Fergus, who operated as The Highlander and had worked with both of the Americans several times, took up his glass and with Skorpion faced their friend with the glasses held out like offerings to a wargod.

When Lastshot turned to Highlander and Skorpion he had a hint of a smile on his lips. "Okay, guys, pour me one; let's drink to a great little lady."

◉◉◉

The Blue Eyed Horse was located in the basement and subbasements of an apartment block off of the *Boulevard Du Lycee*. The eight-story building looked like every other rundown, razor wire-protected slum in the area— except that there were always expensive hovercars parked out front and a squad of well-equipped and highly-paid mercenaries to guard those cars and the people who exited from them.

The Horse was an outlaw club from the very beginning when it was founded in the Eighteen Eighties in a back alley in Marseille. Then it had housed opium dens in its basement, illegal bare knuckle fights in its back salons, and a stable of "working girls" upstairs. The owner, one Anton Leroch, had moved his operation to the Left Bank of the Seine in Paris just before the Nazis had invaded and put him to death. The name of the club had lived on and it had kept its *outre* reputation well into the late twentieth century when its second home had been victim of a firebomb during the first Muslim Uprising.

The new owner had made the unfortunate choice to move to the *Issy Les Moulineaux* area of Paris just before the second Muslim war. What had been a fashionable and quiet apartment complex area had become a war zone and afterward a place that few "fashionable" types had wanted to venture. So the club had changed clientele for a while but not the type and variety of "entertainment" it offered and it was back as a stronghold of darker-focused tastes.

When he was in Paris, Vilna Aurilis always stopped at the "Horse" and used it as an ad hoc office as well as a pleasure center. After he killed the French *Agent Exceptionale* he knew it was the only place he could be sure the police would not pursue him. He knew that there were bribes paid to the right places and Tri V footage of too many high placed officials enjoying the exotic pleasures of the Blue Eyed Horse for there ever to be a raid.

Aurilis was known to Marc, the head of security for the club but still had to be retinal scanned before being admitted through a steel block outer gate that was laser resistant and bulletproof.

Once past the outer gate there was a posh waiting area that concealed several defense devices and automatic gunports; these allowed a single operator in a control room high above in the penthouse of the building to observe and protect the area.

There were several pretty and scantily-clad young men and women in the lounge-like waiting area who greeted the incoming guests. These were rotated frequently so they could not become too familiar with any of the incomers.

Aurilis accepted a mixed drink from one young man and waited for his identity to be confirmed and his payment to be cycled through; no one entered who did not pay.

Another one of the hosts stepped up to the Lithuanian and smiled. "You are confirmed to enter, sir, please come this way." Aurilis could see the small caliber revolver in a hip holster on the host, barely hidden by his skimpy robe.

The arms dealer was lead to an elevator door at the back of the lounge which slid open at his approach. He stepped in and it slid closed. A moment later with no noticeable sensation of descending it slid open to reveal the nearest thing to Sodom the world had to offer.

The Blue Eyed Horse's first level was a hedonist's delight: a recreated Mediterranean environment complete with simulated blue-sky vistas, real marble columned "palaces" and swimming and wading pools.

In and among the simulated Mediterranean ambiance every form of debauchery humans could engage in was being practiced.

Aurilis passed it all by with barely a glance. What he wanted was at the special levels below. A second elevator at the back admitted him to the lower level where he stepped out into a quiet lounge much like a Victorian sitting room.

In the center of it with floating Tri V screens all around him to monitor the action in the club sat the owner and manager of the Blue Eyed Horse, Miloss Skorzny.

"Ah, my friend," Miloss said with a wave of his pudgy hand, "so good to see you again." Miloss Skorzny was a freak: almost five hundred pounds of human flesh that moved like a man a third his size. He was dressed in a blue silk smoking jacket with enough material in it to make a circus tent, and long red hair that flowed over his massive shoulders barely concealing the 'Jack points at his temples. When he smiled his aspect became truly frightening because it revealed his sharp pointed teeth that gave a hint to his own private hobby.

"Miloss," Aurilis said with an answering smile. His host was surrounded by a small crowd of attractive young men and women who were chained at the ankles to his large and comfortable leather easy chair. "I have had quite a day."

"So I heard," the large man said. He stroked one of the women on her back. She seemed to not notice, her eyes clouded by drugs. "I assume you'd like your usual relaxation suite?"

Aurilis smiled again and sighed. "Oh yes," he said, "then I have a Tri V call to make."

Miloss clapped his hands and a liveried manservant appeared out of a side door and beckoned the smuggler. Aurilis followed him down a side corridor that continued the Victorian wood paneled walls and pseudo gas-light feel. At the door marked "seven" the servant stopped and opened the portal, gesturing the guest in.

Aurilis entered and the door was closed behind him.

Inside the Lithuanian stopped and rested his back against the door as he feasted his eyes on the object of his greatest desire. He giggled like a schoolboy and began to remove his clothes.

◎◎◎

"I know I'm asking a lot, Jeremy," Lastshot said, "but she was one of us."

The American and his Scottish friend were seated alone on the roof of the Europack's headquarters with all of nighttime Paris laid out before them.

They had a six-pack of German beer between them as they leaned against the rough stone of an elevator housing. There was a large plastic bowl of potato chips beside the beer that they rummaged around in as they spoke. Both of them stared straight ahead at the lightshow before them, never making eye contact with each other, as if to do so would make them complicit.

"That's true, Conner," the Scottish Exceptional said. "But we shouldn't be having this sort of talk except at the other end of a scrambled com-line," he said. His battle dress uniform was cut along military uniform lines in dark green with plaid accents. He was tall and fair to Lastshot's tall and dark but the two men were clearly of a type.

"I knew the lass personally as well," he said with a tight-lipped whisper. "So we never had this conversation. The Round Table have several of those sort of blind character histories set up around the continent. The one that will probably do you best to "borrow" is a cover identity as a Scottish mil-lionaire and drug dealer named Angus Mac Tavish. "

"Angus?" Lastshot said as he swigged a beer. "Are all you guys cartoons?"

"This from a lad who would wear spurs if they didn't destroy the uphol-stery in his car?" He held out a hand and Lastshot put a can of beer in it.

"But Angus?"

"You'll find the codes for the identity in a file pre-planted on the 'Net for any one of us who fit the description; the whole history is there back to grade school." He munched on some of the chips and washed them down with a healthy swig of the beer. "It seems to me the specs might fit your physical description. It would back up any checks made on him." Lastshot gave a quick smile and emptied his own beer.

The two men stared at the twinkling lights for a long slice of time with-out saying anything. Finally Highlander held up a fresh beer and said, "Grace in her place, an angel gone home. Giulie." He turned the can upside down and let the contents pour out onto the roof.

"She could have been a marine; Giulie." Lastshot followed the Scotsman's lead and up ended his beer as well.

"I'll owe you," the American said.

"No," his companion said, "but this means you have to eat haggis when you stop by London next time."

"Skirt wearin' nutjob," Lastshot said.

"Long haired Cowboy Poff!" Jeremy said with a grin. He turned to look his friend in the eyes and his expression was dead serious again. "Just promise you'll make him hurt."

◎◎◎

The woman called Skorpion and the city of Paris had a long history. And it was a dark one.

After her private drink with Highlander and Lastshot she excused her-self to be alone for a while. She went to the banks of the Seine to walk alone. She wore a long leather duster over her BDU to gain a measure of anonymity. The sound of the city on her right and the gentle lapping of the river along the shore on her left did little to silence the voices and sounds in her head.

Skorpion stared out at the reflections in the water and lit an old fash-ioned cigar. She hated the "new tobacco" cigars that were the rage and had some of the old Havanas she bought from a black marketeer in Tangiers.

They were getting harder to come by.

She puffed on the cigar and hummed to herself to drown out the older sounds and images of the dead French Exceptional so almost didn't hear the mugger because of her preoccupation.

"Give me your money," the harsh voice behind her said.

She turned slowly, angry with herself for being distracted, to face three young men, one of whom was holding an old Glock 17 and pointing it at her head with an unsteady hand. All three muggers had shaven heads and full face tattoos of spiders which marked them as one of the outlaw gangs that roamed the city.

Skorpion scowled at them with annoyance.

"Pick someone else," she said in a growl in gutter French, "I don't want to be bothered to kill you."

The three spiders laughed. One of them, the thinnest who had a double-pierced nose and a slit tongue with rings through it, stepped forward and brandished a long skinning knife.

The redheaded Exceptional moved with blinding speed to snap the knife edge of her right hand into the inside forearm of the forward hand with the blade in it. The bone snapped with an audible "crack." At the same time she sent a sharp bio-electric charge through the shattered bone that would keep it from healing so that he would be maimed for life. She was not in a forgiving mood.

The other two muggers reacted to the pained cry of their friend with curses and threats.

Before they could do anything else Skorpion uncoiled and flicked out her steel whip. The tip wrapped around the body of the automatic and she sent a hard charge down the length of it. When the electric pulse hit the metal hammer on the mostly plastic gun it arced to the primers on the bullets and ignited them so that the gun exploded in the man's hand.

He sank to the ground with a howling cry of agony, clutching the bloody stump of his hand.

The third attacker stared at her, frozen in unbelieving horror and shock as she walked up to him and grabbed his face in her muscular hand. She stared into his eyes and whispered, "Get religion or I will find you and make the rest of your days a nightmare."

The boy ran back up the banks of the river and eventually did get religion.

Skorpion looked at the other two muggers and grunted with satisfaction that their robbery careers were done. Then she looked toward the district where *Le Park* was located and said, "I wish that any of this would have helped you, Giulie. Sorry."

◉◉◉

Lastshot went to his quarters and took a half hour "power" nap before he called up the information that Jeremy had alluded to on his glasses and entered his specifics into the profile, memorizing the preset facts.

The die was cast and his decision was made. He dyed his hair black and speeded up his beard growth so he looked the part to match the profile. Then he quietly slipped out a side door to the hotel he was staying in and headed for *Issey Les Moulineaux.*

He told no one at the Unipol headquarters, particularly not Skorpion, what he was doing. He left his neural glasses behind, disguising his contact points for them as 'net Jack holes.

The cover identity had been planted over two years before but he added his stats so was able to get through the outer gate of the Blue Eyed Horse with no trouble.

Once in the foyer of the club he took a shot of whiskey that was offered to him and did his best not to think about all the guns he had passed to walk into the lion's den.

"Welcome to the Blue Eyed Horse for your first time, sir, my name is Candice." A pretty brunette said to the tall American in accented French. She barely came to his shoulder and made a point of letting him know she had nothing on under her long open front robe. He also noticed she had a pistol strapped to her inner thigh.

"It seems to be quite a place so far, Candice," he said with a slight burr to his voice. "You can call me Angus. It sure seems to be all that was advertised."

"If you will accompany me, Angus," she said, taking his large callused hand gently in her small one. "I will explain the rules of the house." She led him to the elevator at the back of the entrance room and stayed with him as it descended.

"I thought there was nay rules in this place," he said.

"Well," the girl smiled at him, "that is mostly true; with a few exceptions: No images can be recorded or transmitted, though with the blocks on this place that is not likely."

The elevator opened and the two stepped out into a huge open space with raised platforms where booths and tables were set and dark and smoky so that the true dimensions were not visible. The central feature

"Welcome to the Blue Eyed Horse for your first time, sir, my name is Candice."

was an enormous circular dance floor. Off to one side he could see a couple of smaller rooms that seemed miniatures of the main room and had their own entertainments.

"Also, to ease your mind on such matters," Candice continued, "you and everyone who enters this elevator is bio-scanned for contractible diseases and are not allowed to enter our little club if there are any positives. You'll be glad to know you are *very* healthy."

Lastshot acknowledged her statement with a nod and took in the view of the room. He had to work at not being overwhelmed with a sense of disgust at the activity in the room. He was no prude, but he also wasn't all about advertising his private interests.

He smiled down at her and played the part of a sensation hungry rich man. "Ach," he said, "Sure seems it is definitely all I heard of and more."

She smiled at him, her admiration for his obviously muscular build beneath his tailored suit seeming to be very real. "We try. Also no one is allowed to touch any of the staff that are wearing the red armbands—they are security or support. They are also who you can talk to for anything you need or if anyone bothers you. We follow the policy of everything goes and no one is wrong. Nothing that happens in the Blue Eyed Horse is ever talked about outside."

"What's happening?" he asked, noting that all eyes seemed to be directed toward the central area.

"Oh, one of the entertainments is about to begin," she said.

The main dance floor of the club was circular and slightly sunken so the effect was as to make the room into a coliseum. The floor was lit with colored theatrical lights that had shadow-making devices in them that made the floor appear to be a tropical jungle.

"Ladies and gentlemen," the blonde woman in a chariot that was pulled by two other women called out, "The Blue Eyed Horse now presents for your pleasure the race of the sexes. We will round the arena four times and the first chariot to cross the finish line will be declared the winner. The winner will receive a trophy and the loser will have their team sent to the glue factory!" General laughter all around for that. Dancers had set up a cone course around the inner circle of the dance floor so it looked like a real racecourse.

A second chariot pulled by two other women and with a male driver came up beside the first.

"That can't be fair, lassie," Lastshot said.

"Ladies and gentleman," the female charioteer called, "place your bets!"

The betting among the guests was lively, but frivolous. The two carts flew around the ring of the dance floor at a speed that Lastshot would not have thought possible. All the patrons paused in their drinking as the strange race captured all eyes.

The two craft roared around the ring with cheers and hoots from the audience and both charioteers used short whips to spur their charges on.

"*They're really hitting those girls.*" Lastshot did his best to keep his bile from rising as he watched.

Red welts could be seen on the perfect flanks of the women "ponies."

The race however went to the male-driven chariot. And the two women pulling the blonde woman, as they stood panting at the finish line seemed to show real fear in their eyes as she whipped them one last time to have them haul her off.

The audience erupted into a round of applause and Candice smiled at the expression on her charge's face, not realizing it was not startled amazement, but rather guarded disgust.

The "hostess" conducted Lastshot to a small changing room where there were lockers. "You can leave your things here if you so wish and they will, of course, be safe." She stood waiting while he disrobed and placed his clothes in the locker. Her eyes traveled up and down his naked and perfectly muscular form, lingering on the many knife and bullet scars. Her admiration of his naked form was unabashedly frank and her smile inviting.

He returned the look with a smile and took the key from the locker and hung it around his neck on the provided string. He fought his revulsion at what he had seen and the image of the dead Blue Dove to keep "in character."

"*Sometimes going under cover,*" he thought, "*involves no covers at all.*"

"I'm not wearing a red armband," she said as obviously as she could. And by the time she stepped into his arms she was wearing nothing at all.

◉◉◉

The object of Aurilis' lust was a suit. A very special suit.

Outwardly it appeared to be a very realistic, artificial skin horse costume. A Lusitano Stallion just slightly smaller than a full sized beast at ten hands, strong neck, braided mane and shining blue eyes. It was however a state of the art cyber-integrated nano suit. It was an outgrowth of camouflage developed for the military that had been adapted and perverted for the more bizarre tastes of the patrons of the club.

The Lithuanian accepted a drink from a "stable hand" assistant with a relaxed sigh and sipped it. His eyes fixed on the white form suspended before him.

The liquid was neutral tasting. It was actually alive with millions of nanites in solution and would move nanotech monitors throughout his body that would interface with the suit once he was in it. He drained the cup and handed it back to the stablehand.

He was almost shaking with excitement by this point, his breath coming in ragged gasps of excitement. His eyes were shining and he licked his lips frequently with the anticipation of what was to come.

He moved to the underbelly of the great pseudo-stallion and there opened a cleverly concealed entrance portal. He pushed his way up into the belly cavity and slid his arms forward into the spaces in the upper fore-thighs of the horse. The "ribs" the horse sensed his body and wrapped themselves snuggly around his torso as he slid his legs backward to shaped chambers in the upper hind legs.

Warm liquid then filtered in the space all around him that quickly adjusted to be exactly his body temperature so that the sensations of his physical self began to drift away.

It was heaven for Aurilis. He reveled in the complete freedom from his humanity, from the need to make decisions and be in constant control. He knew he was safe at the club, but even more integral to his enjoyment was that he felt supremely safe within his own blue-eyed horse. No one could find him or hurt him in the bosom of the beast.

He did not dwell on much philosophy in his life of crime. He had little time to think about weighty issues beyond day-to-day survival but some part of him wondered if there was a soul and if that soul traveled from form to form. If so, he reasoned he had been a stallion in one of those other lives because it was the only time he was truly at peace.

There was a danger in the total emersion technology; getting lost. Going native, so to speak. Too much time in one of the nano-suits began to alter the neural pathways of the brain and changed how the wearer interfaced with the real world. There had been cases of severe "nano-addiction" where the suit user had gone mad when weaned from the sensation suits. Which is why it had been taken out of military usage—a camo-suit you could only wear for an hour or two was useless in a battlefield situation.

Aurilis always wore it up to the limit. He always did everything up to the limit.

◉◉◉

Lastshot found his guide Candice to be both accomplished and willing in her chosen profession. He allowed himself to enjoy the immediate sensations she provided him, taking a former marine's pride in a "job well done" but never forgot why he was in the modern Sodom. He kept himself alert for any sign of Aurilis or clue to his whereabouts.

"Scotland forever," she said as she rested her head on his chest after some enthusicatic activity. He was reclined against a low couch facing out toward the center of the room.

"It's a matter of national pride," he said in his best imitation of his Highlander friend Jeremy. "It sure is a pretty expensive orgy club." He added, "I had kind of expected—Ah dun know—something more?"

She smiled up at him, running her fingers along the tattoo of the playing card on his chest. "I would have hoped that I was enough," she said coyly.

"Ah, Lassie," he said, "On most days you would be—but with the admission price..." He tried not to make it sound like he was personally disappointed in her performance. She pouted up at the Exceptional and shrugged.

"There is much more here, it is true." She sighed. "In the floor below are many nano suites. And below that"—her expression, despite her professional detachment, darkened and he almost thought he saw fear in her brown eyes—"other things happen. Things I cannot speak of."

"Grand," he said as if he had not noticed her shift in mood, "I think maybe I'd like to take a peep of these nano suites, if that's permitted."

Her smile returned and her eyes brightened. "I can show you." She stood up and grabbed his hand to pull him to his feet. Lastshot allowed himself to be pulled along, eyes still scanning every naked, writhing form in the room as he moved across it toward the rear elevator.

"I'll find you/Aurilis," he thought. "Somehow I'll find you."

◉◉◉

"Welcome to my little establishment, Mr. MacTavish," Miloss Skorzny said to the naked Exceptional. The "disguised" Lastshot was standing with Candice in the central reception area of the second level of the Blue Eyed Horse.

"It sure is something," Lastshot said. "But I heard that you have these special rooms down here?" He saw a look pass between the giant man and the naked girl who stood beside him. "She's terrified of this freak," he thought, "not just pimp and working girl scared." And he could understand why. He looked into the drugged eyes of the chained figures at the massive pimp's feet. *"I have to find a way to shut this place down after I get the Lithuanian. That will be a service to humanity."*

"We do our humble best to make it a memorable experience for all our customers," the host said, "and yes, this floor has some lovely nano suites. Why don't you head back up stairs, Candice, my dear, I will talk to you later."

Lastshot could feel her shudder through the hand she held his with.

"Sure, Monsieur Skorzny," she said with a voice that showed no strain at all, "I will see you later, Angus."

"See you later, lassie," he said. And he meant it. Lastshot watched the shapely behind of the girl as she walked with a quick step toward the elevator. He knew she was a prostitute and had no illusions about saving every one he met, but he would make sure she did not suffer because he had gotten information out of her that her boss did not want to share.

He turned back to watch the massive Miloss as he scanned the many screens before him. He took note of the pointed teeth and the net jacks and marked the man as one of the most dangerous he had ever met.

"I think down that hall, room five will be a nice start for you, Mr. MacTavish," Skorzny said, "I'm sure a nano trip to space will be delightful: I hear Zero G sex is amazing." He smiled to showcase his fangs.

"Fab!" Lastshot said. He walked down the corridor without a look back.

It was unfortunate that he didn't because at that moment Aurilis entered the reception area from another corridor and saw the naked Exceptional as he exited the area. A wide smile lit the blonde's face as he stepped up to Miloss' chair.

"My friend, Miloss," he said, "I have something to tell you and then a Tri V call to make—I think I have solved a problem for you and one for me at the same time."

◉◉◉

Conner Lastshot walked down the corridor toward the door marked number five with a foreboding of something being wrong. In all his years in the military and then law enforcement he had relied on those "gut feelings" to keep alive.

Now he was walking naked down a dark corridor three levels below a fortress-like entrance with no chance of back up. He knew his transponder would not register from so shielded an area. His only chance for a rescue if things went bad was the note he had left to be delivered to Skorpion at lunchtime the next day. He knew that by then it would be good or done for him. Game over.

"*Maybe Red was not so chicken in telling me to back off,*" he thought.

He arrived at the door and stopped for a moment to take a deep breath. He activated his implants to inject a trace amount of Regen into his system to give him the best reflexive edge he could get on opening the door.

Then he grasped the knob and entered.

◎◎◎

"You got some nerve calling me, you stinking filthy cheat." "Mickey" Michencko spoke with a contained fury that the Holographic image and distance to Moscow did nothing to diminish.

Vilna Aurilis was in a holo-suite in the second level of the Blue Eyed Horse so he could make a Tri V connection with the Russian gang boss.

"You are right to be upset," the Lithuanian said, "I know we did not have a good deal last time—"

"Good deal?" the little mobster snarled, "You cost me two hundred millions and a lot of good will!" He leaned into the vid lens and whispered through grinding teeth, "I will have you turned inside out while you are still alive for that."

Aurilis did his best to hold his expression steady in the face of so virulent a tirade. He knew his only chance to avoid the Russian's fury was to give him something he was even more angry at and potentially worth more than what he had lost.

"Yes, I am sure you can arrange that with no difficulty," Aurilis said, "but I may have some one you would like to do that to even more."

"You can not talk your way out of—"

"Lastshot." Aurilis interjected, "the man who caught my fellow Lithuanian, Kidolis last year."

This stopped the little criminal in mid word. He stared at the vid lens slack jawed and then whispered. "Lastshot. You can get me Lastshot?"

"I have him," Aurilis exaggerated, "here at the Blue Eyed Horse."

Michencko sat back, his features unreadable but he breathed out hard between his clenched teeth. "If you lie I will make your death even more horrible." He stroked the horse statue on his desk with a loving caress.

"I have made one mistake in not being truthful with you," the Lithuanian smuggler admitted. "Even I am not so stupid to do it twice."

The far away mobster smiled a tight-lipped smile. "I will forget the incident about the rail guns if I have Lastshot alive for my uses at my farm in Vilnius in twenty four hours."

"I will take care of all the shipping," Aurilis said, a second inspiration lighting his face, "And I am sure you will love how he is delivered."

◉◉◉

Lastshot was surprised when he entered the room. It was a large stainless steel room with a bay window that gave the illusion of looking out onto a recreation of the launch pad for the Japanese Mars Launch that landed men on the red planet for the first time. The immediate area he entered was a staging area near the door where a space suit hung in a rack. There was also a beautiful Japanese girl in a flight attendant's uniform.

"Good evening, sir," she said in French. "If you will don your flight attire we will get you into orbit on your way as soon as possible; your female crew is waiting for you."

The puzzled Exceptional let her begin to help him into the old spacesuit. This was a process like a knight donning armor so he had to stand in place as she helped him step into the boot connected to the one-piece suit.

He looked down at her smiling, almond-eyed face as she knelt to help him step into the clumsy boots and whistled softly. "This is getting to be a hard assignment," he thought with a wry smile, "but I had better play my part or they'll—"

Suddenly the door the room exploded inward and five body armorwearing figures charged into the room. They were holding Kaiser-Mitland stun rifles that fired glass globes of electrical discharge. They leveled them at the Exceptional.

Lastshot acted instantaneously. His implants speeded his reflexes and he grabbed the startled attendant, pulling her up to block the first rifle discharge with her body. The girl fell like a marionette whose strings had been cut but her hour of sleep bought the Exceptional the time he needed to disengage from the boots.

The American snatched up the helmet from the spacesuit and used it like a shield, taking the next two shots from the rifles he knew were in position to shoot. It allowed him to get close enough to the first shooter to grab the gun barrel and twist it free from the man's grasp.

Lastshot swung the space helmet with enough force to crack both it and the helmet of the disarmed gunman. The man's body blocked a clear shot from the other shooters and Lastshot used the time that gave him to reverse the stun rifle.

He slammed a hard front snap front kick into the disarmed attacker that drove the man into the two gunmen directly behind.

"Lousy tactical deployment" he thought, as he chambered a stun round.

Lastshot followed the kicked gunman forward and charged the two still on their feet. He fired the stun rifle for effect aiming for their face shields. He knew that the electrical discharge would not penetrate their armor but would make it impossible for them to see clearly.

The gunmen were not idle, however. They were also firing for effect.

Lastshot knew they would try for body shots so he snatched up the spacesuit and held it before him. The material of the suit not only absorbed the impact of the glass capsules that contained the static charge but also dissipated most of the charge.

The hand holding the suit went quickly numb from the charge but it allowed him to get close enough to swing the rifle and crack the faceplate of the nearest gunman. As the man dropped Lastshot side-kicked past him and broke the thigh of the last gunman.

The last man screamed in pain that was stopped abruptly as Lastshot vaulted past him and added an elbow to his faceplate as a *coup de grace*.

As the American dove past he pulled the now unconscious man's side-arm from his holster, discarding the stun rifle.

Lastshot dove through the open door into the hallway rolling behind the two guards that had been stationed as a rearguard.

The American came up firing. He could feel the weight of the ammo and knew it must be armor piercing.

The two guards were overwhelmed by the speed of the attack. They turned to try to bring their rifles to bear but he took them both out with single shots through their face shields.

He was on his feet before they hit the carpet, snatching up a second sidearm from one of them and moving back toward the elevator.

"There must be an emergency exit from this cesspool," he thought, *"for fire and in the unlikely event of a police raid but I don't have time to really look for it."* The fact that he was naked in the stronghold of a madman with armed thugs all around him was not even a real concern for Lastshot. *"I have to find that scum Aurilis."*

One of the doors opened and an older distinguished man with a long grey mustache stepped into the hall. He was stark naked and holding the hand of a short fat woman in a nun's habit.

"Nice to see you, sister," Lastshot quipped as he ran past the startled pair,

"I'll be late with my history assignment."

The Exceptional emerged into the reception area of the floor and spotted Aurilis standing beside the massive seated form of Skorzny.

When the Lithuanian saw the frightening figure of the naked, gun-toting Exceptional race into the area he screamed and turned on his heels to run for the elevator .

Lastshot was in no mood to waste time so he snapped off a shot that put a bullet cleanly through Aurilis' left thigh.

"You bastard!" The Lithuanian screamed as he hit the ground. "You shot me." The smuggler whimpered while he tried to stop the tide of blood from his punctured thigh.

The Exceptional ran up to him and placed one of the automatics directly on the man's temple. "You are going to stand trial or you are going to die right here," he said. "You have the choice; don't matter one way or the other to me."

Before the smuggler could answer, five hundred pounds of solid muscle slammed into The Exceptional and sent him careening end over end across the lobby.

Lastshot lost both the pistols in the uncontrolled tumble.

When he got oriented and tried to rise, the massive Miloss was on him with pounding fists that were like iron. The first two punches broke Lastshot's nose and knocked a tooth loose.

The former marine didn't need the drugs he pumped into his system to kill the pain or amp his strength; he was angry at being hit and madder than hell at being denied his prey. Lastshot shot a knee into the pimp's groin.

The giant evidenced absolutely no reaction to the strike save to throw his head back and laugh. Lastshot then launched a chop kick from the ground driving the instep of his foot into the exposed throat of the man mountain.

Miloss choked hard and the Exceptional pressed his advantage driving two punches into the man's Adam's apple. Skorzny staggered back, his eyes watering as he gasped for breath.

Lastshot got to his feet, ignoring the blood streaming from his shattered nose. He picked up one of the automatics and grabbed the still whimpering Aurilis by his collar.

"Give me a reason and I *will* blow your face off." Lastshot said. He went straight to the elevator and noticed that the indicator showed that it was on the way down.

The Exceptional spotted Aurilis standing beside the massive form of Skorzny.

"You'll never make it out of here, Exceptional!" Aurilis said.

"Shut up, loser. I can carry you just as easy as you can hop." Lastshot stepped back and trained his gun on the sliding doors of the lift in anticipation of more trouble.

The elevator stopped and the door opened. Instead of armed troops only the girl Candice was inside.

"Quickly," she said, "come in here; I was watching on the security monitors."

Lastshot stepped in pulling the Lithuanian behind him and looked back to see the massive Miloss getting to his feet with a furious expression on his distorted face. Beyond the pimp he saw more shock troops racing into the lobby.

"Is there another way out up top—" he began to say but never finished because the girl slammed a stun baton into his back and jolted Lastshot into unconsciousness with fifty thousand volts.

◉◉◉

Conner Le'Schott woke up in a great deal of pain. He was disoriented and felt very strange.

His vision was consisted only of shapes and colors and the sounds that came to his ears was dull and thrumming.

He tried to speak, if only to hear the sound of his own voice but no sound came out. His throat was parched and he had a metallic taste in it.

He tried to move but couldn't.

For a long space of time he had trouble remembering what exactly had happened but the pain he felt in his side and his face recalled the fight with the massive Skorzny and his backing into the elevator.

"The girl?" he thought. "It had to be the girl."

The muffled sounds that came to him began to resolve themselves into human voices and then specific words became decipherable.

"It is the perfect way to transport him," Aurilis' voice said with a plaintive tone to it.

"I want to see him suffer personally," the hoarse voice of Skorzny said, "I want to eat his organs and taste his heart while he watches me do it."

"I know, Miloss," Aurilis said. Now his voice was a little desperate as well as cajoling, "and I want him to have a world of pain as well, but if Michencko doesn't get him to do the exact same thing to him we want to, more or less, I am a dead man." The large man made a grunting sound. "But I am sure he will give you tapes of his demise and…and maybe even send you all the parts for a nice snack after the fact."

The sounds became less muffled and the blurry images before his eyes became the distorted shapes of the two felons. Standing with them was the girl Candice, looking subdued.

"Well," Skorzny said, "I suppose that will do. We can't have him killing you, Vilna, you are one of the few clients here who make me laugh." The big man chuckled then and the Lithuanian joined him with a nervous giggle.

"I did all right?" Candice asked. She had trouble looking over at the captive Exceptional and kept her eyes averted toward the floor.

The big man put a massive hand around the girl's shoulders. "Little Candice, you came through for me, despite my earlier disappointment in you." He bent down and planted a wet kiss on the girl's cheek. "You might even get a bonus if you can make Vilna here forget his painful leg by the end of the evening."

She perked up then and smiled over at the blonde arms dealer.

"When this law pig is wrapped up for shipping I'll be glad to help Candice earn her bonus," Aurilis said. He moved closer to Lastshot and the American realized he was bound to a table-like device in a darkened room.

Beyond the three criminals Lastshot could see several odd shapes in racks along the walls; they seemed to be animals of various sorts—unicorns, griffins, lions and horses. And stranger shapes he could not identify.

"He's awake," Aurilis said. "How delightful." He stepped close and launched an open-handed slap across Lastshot's face.

The American's vision swam again and blurred to red.

"I want you to know what is going to happen to you, Exceptional," Aurilis said. "I am going to turn you into an animal and send you to a very angry little man in Moscow who is going to hurt you very badly."

A second slap sent the America into blackness once more.

The next time Lastshot came to consciousness he was being lifted bodily by several muscular men from the table and carried across the room to one of the four-legged shapes hanging from harnesses on the wall.

He was vaguely aware of Aurilis watching with an almost fevered glow to his face, his eyes shining with anticipation.

"I'm gonna remember you," Lastshot thought.

They carried him to the underbelly of one of the horses, a great white beast, superbly molded to a lifelike reality that would have defied any but the most detailed examination to discover was an imitation. The men who handled the Exceptional were none too gentle in their manipulations and bodily shoved him up into the belly of the equine, strapping him in.

When they withdrew their hands there was a moment when Lastshot thought he might be able to wiggle free, to make one last attempt to fight his way out of whatever fate they had for him but then the tendrils of the horse's ribs enclosed him and he knew he was trapped.

He distantly heard the sound of the belly being sealed, a hissing sound that was as final as the clanging of a steel door on death's row. Then he felt a liquid begin to fill the spaces around his naked flesh and there was a moment of claustrophobic panic.

He knew that one of the most tried and true torture and interrogation techniques used on prisoners was water boarding. It was means by which the torturer simulated drowning the victim by holding him or her upside down and pouring water through a cloth on their face. It was a frightening experience, one that Lastshot had endured in his training for the Marine Corps and actually had once had done to him on a black ops mission.

He was afraid that they were torturing him with another method, however, one even more terrifying: actually drowning and revival. It took a terrible toll on the victim and eventually the body of the person being put through it gave out from the strain. It was all Lastshot could do to fight the natural panic in him that rose with volume of liquid around him.

In the darkness of the space he had been shoved in his face came in contact with a molded surface and he felt a puff of air on his cheek. He pushed his face forward and felt it come to rest in a mask-like cradle with a space for his nose and eyes to rest.

He blinked and the eyes gave him a view of the room he had just been in where the men who had placed him in the horse were filing out to leave only Miloss, Aurilis and one muscular attendant. He realized that he was seeing through the eyes of the horse he had been encased in and drawing breath through some sort of tube arrangement that let him breath, possible through the horse's mouth.

"*So they don't plan to kill me,*" he thought, "*at least not just yet.*"

The liquid filled the space all around his battered body and soon he began to lose sensation in his body, as if in an isolation tank. He moved his head and the vision field from out of the horse's head shifted. He could see the girl Candice standing reluctantly by the door to the room.

"I see he is awake and can see us," Miloss said. He grinned to show his sharpened teeth. Lastshot could see that there was a long bruise on the left side of the massive man's face and the thought that he had given it to the pimp gave him a small sense of satisfaction.

"Hello, Mr. Lastshot," the giant said, "I hope you will recover fully from our little dance; I wouldn't want you to miss one single sensation that is about to come your way in your new life."

Aurilis, standing beside the man mountain, leaning on a crutch for support, laughed in a high-pitched chuckle. "Welcome to your own personal hell, may you live in it for a long time."

The words of both men came clearly to the American's ears and they chilled him. He was truly on his own and in the grip of the most evil men in the world.

His descent into hell had only just begun.

⊙⊙⊙

The two master criminals could not send their prisoner on to his fate in Russia without indulging their own perverted desires for revenge a little first. Lastshot did his best to resist, but he was not fully in control of the large nano-linked body so his attempts to be disagreeable were weak. Ultimately the Exceptional also knew there was little point in protesting just to protest.

Skorzny sat on a reinforced bench just outside a practice ring munching on a sandwich of some unidentifiable meat while Aurilis leaned on the inner railing of the working area as if afraid he would miss some detail of the faux training session.

Candice sat sullenly a little behind the men averting her eyes. She looked up at the spectacle before her only when one of the men drew her attention to some nuance of the exhibition.

A groom applied the whip to the flanks of the faux horse liberally as he led it through a series of exercises for the private audience. Inside the nano-suit Lastshot continued to be surprised that he could feel the sting of the lash each time.

He had known of the camo-suits, at least of the pared down versions that had been put into general use for covert operations, but had no idea that they had developed to such an astoundingly detailed level. The fact that he could "feel" the welts the whip raised began to prey on his mind. He did not realize that these sensory overwhelms had been the very reason that only "stripped down" version of the suit had ever made it to the field.

Lastshot felt, or imagined he felt, sweat rising from the exertion of the session. His already sore muscles began to ache as if he had been running a race or working out with weights. He knew that it had to be a mentally created sensation, that is, he imaged it was happening so his muscles twitched and responded as if it was, like a sleeper with an active dream whose muscles cycled through, in a minor way, the actions he was actually dreaming about.

Aurilis watched the prancing of the pseudo-horse with the fascination of a mongoose watching a cobra. He recalled his own moments in the suit not so long before and laid those feelings over the scenario before him. He eyes were wide and his mouth hung slack. His breath was is short, shallow gasps that were almost exclamations of excitement.

Miloss took notice.

"Would you like to take him for a little ride before we crate him for travel?" the massive man asked.

The Lithuanian took a moment to disengage his eyes from the vision before him. When he turned to the pimp there was still a faraway look in them. "Yes," he said, "I would like that."

There was an element of deep hatred in his voice, but not from the fact that the Exceptional had put a bullet in his leg or caused him embarrassment in front of Miloss; it was that the prisoner was experiencing what he himself could not, the complete subjugation of his conscious mind to the equine form.

Inside the suit Lastshot was having trouble distinguishing reality.

Unlike Aurilis who had worn the suit many times and craved it, the American was feeling his sense of self erode more quickly and with no clear boundary to his imprisonment in sight, the utter hopelessness was numbing his mind more swiftly. He was only vaguely aware of the weight of the saddle on "his" back and was not quite sure what was going on until he saw the arms dealer hobble up beside him.

When he felt the full weight of the Lithuanian on his back Lastshot decided not to react. He was getting the feel of his new, huge body and he knew his mind was slipping away through the synaptic connectors that linked him to it.

"That's the way, Vilna!" Miloss yelled. He washed down the sandwich with a jug of Basque wine. He clapped his pudgy hands in delight as the rider became more confident and began to push his charge into more complicated maneuvers.

Candice watched with a face that was trying to be stoic but was washed with waves of revulsion that she could not hide. She kept her hands in her lap like a schoolgirl forced to watch a play and said nothing.

"I told you we could turn him into an animal!" Aurilis called out, "See, ha! I feel like John Wayne!"

At the mention of his hero that Blue Dove had nicknamed him, Lastshot decided he had lulled the rider into a false sense of security long enough and bucked. He whirled. He kicked out hitting one of the grooms with a slashing hoof and opened a bloody gash in the man's head.

The attendants raced and tried to get a line on the half ton of fury but Lastshot had "figured out" his new body well enough to avoid them and still keep the Lithuanian on his back in screaming terror.

The horse attendants got two ropes around the mad prisoner's "neck" and were able to steady his whirling antics enough for Aurilis to attempt to jump off. He was hampered by his wounded leg, however and paused at the moment of the jump.

Lastshot sensed him about to leave his back and bucked hard, like an exaggerated shudder which flung the half dismounted man from his back with such force that Aurilis hurt his good leg when he landed.

Aurilis was so furious at his new injury that he almost shot the trapped Exceptional in the suit until Miloss prevailed on him to not cause his own demise by the act.

"Think, my friend," the massive man said. "As you have counseled me, he will be punished and your debt will be cleared. Better to be doubly revenged."

Lastshot was to be secured for travel by simply holding a canister of drugs up to the nose of the horse suit that he would be forced to inhale it. Then he was to be secured in the harness internally with his face held against the breathing/viewing mask.

The servomotor in the suit would prevented him from falling over so that he would sleep much as a real horse would, standing up. By use of cranes and slings they would then pack the pseudo-equine in a travel pod like a real horse for air transport.

Miloss and Aurilis stood before the trapped man and gloated.

"I want you to know, lawman," the Lithuanian said with a sneer, "just what hell you are going to." He winced as he leaned on one of the naked helpmates Miloss had provided for him. "I've sold you to 'Mickey' Michencko, cop. And what he will do to you will—"

Suddenly a claxon sounded.

"What is that?" Aurilis yelled.

Miloss moved with surprising speed for a man of his bulk, whirling from the horse-suited man and moved toward a wall panel. "We've been breeched," he yelled back at Aurilis. "We have to use my escape route."

Before he could input a full code the door at the other end of the room exploded inward.

Skorpion stepped through the doorway, a submachine gun in each hand. She was dressed in her full Exceptionals regalia, all in shades of red, from the deep maroon of the symbol-incised leather bodice to the bright scarlet of her wide belt that was embossed with a figure of a scorpion. Even without the belt it was obvious that she could not be codenamed anything else for her face was decorated with a scorpion tattoo on its left side.

Miloss made a sound like a surprised cat and seized one of his sycophant slaves to physically throw at the Exceptional.

Skorpion dodged nimbly and fired past the screaming naked boy, her shot taking the giant in his right shoulder to spin him around.

Aurilis tried to get away from Lastshot toward another door but the trapped Exceptional, even disoriented, sensed the movement and snapped the horse head around hard to connect with the Lithuanian's shoulder. This sent the man stumbling forward to the floor.

"You in there, Lastshot?" the redhead called.

The trapped Exceptional nodded his faux head.

In a moment Skorpion had raced across the room to reach under the stallion suit to hit the release. There was a hiss and suddenly Lastshot felt a rush of sensation. He dropped from the cavity in the belly to land with a wet thump on the floor.

Aurilis howled and crawled toward a far door.

Skorpion yelled, "Stop moving, scumbag!"

The moaning Miloss had recovered his feet now and launched himself at the redhead.

The two of them slammed to the ground and the massive pimp got his muscular arms around her neck. He opened his mouth and began to bite her with his filed teeth.

Lastshot worked to come out of his semi-coma when he saw his friend in danger but his physical disorientation kept him weak and made it hard to focus.

Skorpion was pinned beneath Miloss, her arms trapped beneath her. He pulled back on her head and worked to get his teeth at her exposed throat.

Aurilis made it to his feet and limped for the door again, but then saw one of the guns that had flown out of Skorpion's hands on the floor. He went for it.

"Conner!" Skorpion yelled at the same time she slammed her head back into Miloss's face.

Aurilis grabbed the gun. Lastshot exploded from the ground and flew across the room to tackle the Lithuanian.

Aurilis tried to bring the gun up to bear but Lastshot, holding the barrel, stopped him by punching him in the fresh leg wound.

Aurilis screamed.

Lastshot yanked the gun from him, spun and shot Miloss clean through the left shoulder.

Just then another tactical team from the Blue Eyed Horse charged into the room from one of the corridors and seeing their boss on the ground tried to move to get a clear shot at the red clad Exceptional.

Lastshot took the opportunity to fire four rapid fire shots into the face-plates of the new arrivals before they realized he was a danger.

Skorpion rolled out from under the screaming, pimp and slammed an elbow into the side of his head to put him out cold.

"You have to get me a doctor," Miloss yelled.

"Shut up," she said and sent a stunning electrical jolt into the mountain of flesh that quieted him.

Lastshot used the gun to cover the hallway in the event of other arrivals. "You have good ideas, Red," he said. "And not to sound ungrateful, but... how?"

Skorpion took off her over robe and tossed it to the naked Exceptional who donned it. She tossed him his neural glasses as well and he snapped them into place with relief. Once he heat scanned he saw no more danger up the hall.

Aurlis moaned and Lastshot kicked him in the hip and pointed the gun at him. The Lithuanian quickly quieted.

"Highlander," Skorpion said, "finally confessed to me that he'd given you the cover identity, so I realized the only way to proceed was directly. I enlisted the Blue Dove's teammates from Unipol for a long overdue raid on the Blue Horse. They had a tactical plan for this for a long time, but no political will to execute it 'til now."

"There are enough bad guys here to justify it to their higher ups," Lastshot said. "Hell, half of the higher ups are probably here."

"You know cowboys are supposed to ride on top of the horse," Skorpion said.

"The cavalry is supposed to wear blue," he said.

"Ungrateful swine," she said to her naked partner. "But you do have nice legs."

"Just nice legs?"

"Professional detachment," she said. "Now let's go finish closing this place down before you ask me that again."

"There is a girl here named Candice," he said, "who can—"

"I don't want to know."

"Just saying."

"Another of your lost causes?"

He gave her a sour look. "I just feel a bit responsible for her—even if she did me dirty."

"Okay, John Wayne," Skorpion said, "let's go head them off at the pass then maybe take a walk in the park."

And the two Exceptionals went out to finish the job the Blue Dove had started. They then took a walk to a spot in the park where she fell and drank a round to her memory.

The End

◉◉◉

Teel James Glenn has stories have been printed in magazines from *Weird Tales, Spinetingler, SciFan, Mad, Black Belt, Fantasy Tales, Pulp Empire, Sherlock Holmes Mystery, SciFan, Sixgun Western, Crimson Streets, Silver Blade Quarterly, Tales of Old, Blazing Adventures* and scores of other publications and dozens of books and anthologies in many genres. His short story "The Clockwork Nutcracker" won best steampunk story for 2013 from Preditor and Editors poll.

He is also the winner of the 2021 Best Novel for *A Cowboy in Carpathia: A Bob Howard Story* and the 2012 Pulp Ark Award for Best Author, his website is: TheUrbanSwasbuckler.com

RISE OF THE BUND
A KIRI ADVENTURE

By Curtis Fernlund

Union Square
New York City
May 1, 1937

"**W**hy's it so crowded? I hate this."

"Stop grousing, Stubby and try to keep up."

Denise Pulitzer held tight onto Stewart 'Stubby' Stubbins camera strap and continued to drag him along through the tight-pressed crowd. She felt like grousing herself however, at her mother for saddling her with the complaining 'shutterbug' to cover this story. She was no slouch with a camera, a fact she had proven over and over and her mother knew that. But Denise knew her mother always had some ulterior motive, and was always trying to 'broaden Denise' horizons' in the process; trying to mold the Cub Reporter into a first class journalist capable of one day handling all the aspects of the Pulitzer Media Empire. But it was so infuriating at times, Denise wanted to scream.

It wasn't Stubby's fault she knew. She was actually quite fond of the guy, she really was. Stewart "Stubby" Stubbins was a queer little fellow, but she just had to love him. He was short and chubby, but cute; sort of a cross between Lou Costello and Curly Howard. Not Denise' first choice for a dream date of course, but he had a heart of gold, and despite a long streak of bad luck and a perpetual state of clumsiness, he could always make her smile. Stubby often accompanied reporters in the field, carrying radio equipment along with his own camera, driving the car and the like. He had a regular job with *World News Radio*: Stubby acting as a soundman for 'On-the-Spot' reporters. He was also a free-lance shutterbug, usually selling his photos to the *New York World*, the paper that owned the radio station, a newer branch of her mother's empire.

He was right about one thing though; it was a huge crowd. It always was though. Every year on May First people of all races from all around the Tri-State Area and beyond gathered in Manhattan's Union Square to rally for the cause of the 'Working Man'. Denise knew from her research the movement really got started back in the late 1800's not long after the Civil War. They came out in droves to protest for equality in the work-place; a decent wage, better working conditions, child-labor laws. A lot of people died in those early protests turned riots. They often got out of control and many times back then the police were just as lawless as the people they were there to supposedly 'serve and protect'. Denise knew if not for the labor movement and the unions she'd probably be working alongside dozens of other women in some sweat shop laundry or sewing factory sixteen hours a day for some pittance of pay like they did back in the early years of the Twentieth Century.

Well, maybe not her. As the potential heiress of the Pulitzer Fortune and Media Empire she was far better off than most young women her own age. Even as a child she wanted for nothing; went to the best schools and learned all the courtly graces, such as they were here in New York's Society. She had all the finest teachers her grandfather and mother could afford to hire or buy; though of course her best teacher throughout her youth, and still was Suwan Shinobi.

Suwan was her mother's best friend and *confidante* as they called it back in the last century; the Victorian Age. She had become Denise's fast friend and mentor over the years growing up as well. Suwan was always there it seemed; oh, not hovering over her like a mother hen, but never far away with a word of advice or caution at the proper time, like when to cross the street or stay out of the poisonous cleaning supplies cabinet. She never seemed to be watching but Denise remembered too many times like when she had fallen roller skating or skinned her knee playing Hop-Scotch Suwan was immediately at her side with a comforting word and hug drying her eyes. In many ways Suwan Shinobi was almost more of a mother to her than her true mother.

Diane Pulitzer was a wonderful woman and she too taught Denise so very much growing up and she truly cared. But Diane was an up-and-coming journalist when they all were younger and she spent many hours at Joseph Pulitzer's newspaper, the *New York World*. She wanted to be the best, Denise new that now, but there were times when she wanted—needed her mother. Luckily Suwan had been there as well. And speaking of which…

"Suwan, are you still with us?" Denise called back over her shoulder above the din of the rowdy crowd. Even as she was turning to look however, Suwan was right there at her side, as always.

"I'm here," she replied scanning the mob warily, "though I wish none of us were. I agree with Mister Stubbins; it's far too crowded to be safe and with the growing warmth, tempers are too short and ready to flare. We should be elsewhere or at least on the fringes and not in the thick of things."

"Nonsense," Denise dismissed with a wave and a smile, "we need to get closer to hear what the speakers have to say. Despite that bull-horn they're using I can't make out a word. Now c'mon," she insisted as she shoved through the crowd trying to move closer to the makeshift stage at the edge of the park; little more than a soapbox with a table cobbled together in front of it. Hardly a speaker's podium, she mused, but they were all exercising their First Amendment Rights, assembling to peacefully protest and speaking their minds freely. Just as I'm using my Freedom of the Press, she mentally added.

Denise received many a complaint and mumbled curse though as she continued to weave a path for the three of them through the throng. Everyone it seemed wanted to be at the forefront of the action, no one wanting to be shoved aside and lose their spot. Signs were waving sporting slogans; Better Wages, Shorter Hours and Improved Working Conditions, though some were far more colorful in their language than others. Too she saw placards and banners touting words in languages she could not begin to comprehend. New York City was often dubbed the 'Melting Pot of the World' and it was never so evident as when the people of the city gathered to protest, no matter the reason.

She could hear Stubby snapping pictures all along as he followed, doing his job using his trusty Kodak. She had no worries on that front. Stubby was a top-notch photographer and always seemed to get the best shots, often far superior to her own she hated to admit. It was a pity he did not have his radio broadcast equipment with him today but his usual cohort, Lisa Lord of the *World News Radio,* was off in New Jersey with another Sound Crew at a similar event.

"Hey! Watch who you're shovin', girlie!"

Denise came up short as a tall, gruff man suddenly reared up in front of her. He was an ugly cuss, she thought, with a huge, red-veined nose and scruffy lantern jaw. His suit seemed old and worn, a blue, double-breasted pinstripe that had seen better days. He was carrying a sign nailed to a stout pole, which might easily be turned into a club if this peaceful rally boiled over into a riot.

"I'm sorry," Denise offered raising her hands apologetically to ward him off. "I was just trying to get closer to the speaker. I can't hear..." Denise was about to pull out her Press Pass for the *World* but the man gave her no time.

"Ya wanna hear, toots," the man growled brandishing his sign. Denise saw the word 'Jew' scrawled on the board. "Well, now hear this!"

Denise tried to back away as the sign swung at her but she thumped up against Stubby right on her heels. She raised her arms to ward off the blow but knew it would do little good. The man was huge compared to her. This was going to hurt.

And of course Suwan was there.

Suwan stepped in front of Denise; her own arms raised defensively as the sign came crashing down. She blocked with her forearm, her ever-present wrist bracer absorbing the blow as she deflected it down and to the side. She continued her movement though, her long hours, years of training taking over as she stepped into the man and spun bringing her arm full circle to smash the back of her fist into the side of the brute's face.

Denise yelped at the ferocity of the sudden scene even as the man's head twisted to the side. He grunted and pink spittle flew with the impact forcing him to stagger. He shook his head as Suwan stepped around and shoved the man into the crowd. He didn't fall in the tight-packed mob but immediately Denise heard raised voices over what happened.

"Hey! Watch it!"

"Watch who yer shovin'!"

"Chink!"

"Slant!"

"Weiblich Hund!"

That from a man, catching Denise' attention. He was tall and fair-haired but dressed oddly for a peaceful rally in this crowd and heat; a black, long-sleeved shirt and tan jodhpurs, with black leather riding boots all prim, proper and polished. He had a look of rage twisting his face and Denise quickly saw he was not alone as there were at least a dozen others dressed exactly like he was.

Denise Pulitzer was no fool. She knew what this was and who those men must be. She had listened to her mother, Diane drone on and on over the growing war in Europe. Starting with that queer little German's rise to power when Adolf Hitler was appointed Chancellor back in 1933, then just last year the county's armies invading the Rhineland along with Italy conquering Ethiopia. There was news of unrest in Russia as well, and only last March her mother and Kiri the Mist encountered the German *Bund* trying to blow up the Empire State Building. It seemed the war was coming to America and these men were Nationalist supporters of Aryan Germany, the *Blackshirts* she had seen in so many Newsreels at the cinema. These were even wearing the telltale red armbands emblazoned with the Nazi Swastika.

"Uhh, Miss Denise…" Denise felt Stubby grabbing her arm but she shrugged his grip away. "We should get out of here. This looks bad."

"Get that, Stubby!" she ignored him pointing at the Nazi supporters shouting over the growing din as the men started to surge forward. Her own safety cast aside, this was about to become news and she wanted the story. "Get that shot!"

Sudden movement caught her attention as the first man regained his footing and ripped the placard from his sign post, brandishing it like a club at Suwan. He shouted something foul now sounding German and swung his stick like a bat. Suwan was swift to counter though and Denise saw her as her body seemed to physically change.

No longer defensive, she stepped to the side avoiding the wild blow and caught the man's arm within the crook of her own. She shifted her weight and tugged the larger brute off balance pulling him forward with his own momentum then brought her other forearm down on the back of his neck when he bent. At the same time she brought her leg up and drove the man's face squarely into her thrusting knee. Denise heard something crunch and the man squealed before Kiri shoved him to the ground at her feet. He hit hard and blood spattered the pavement from his shattered nose. He struggled to rise for a moment then collapsed.

Seeing that the Nazis became really enraged. They shouted and cursed as they surged forward, their own signs now bludgeons and clubs raised high in anger. Denise heard Stubby yelling behind her as he grabbed her arm again and this time she stumbled back as he tried to pull her away from the advancing mob. At the same time Kiri was in front of her, her body flowing soft and gracefully like the mist she named herself after.

She stepped right into the mob of Blackshirts without concern to her own safety slapping away the clubs and tripping up the angered Nazi supporters. Denise could tell she was not trying to hurt them as she moved, dancing to some tune only she could hear. She saw one young man fall to the ground while another had his baton stripped away in a fluid move too swift to follow. Now with a weapon Denise heard wood striking wood like the sound of bats swinging, hitting for the 'Nickel Bleachers'. Another Blackshirt went to his knees and another doubled over as the wind gushed out of him. And then Stubby was in front of her.

He was taking pictures frantically as he tried to move Denise back while standing in front of her to keep her out of harm's way, bless him. Denise was just like her mother however, and no stranger to danger. This was news exploding right before her as the peaceful rally suddenly turned ugly. She saw most of the rest of the crowd backing away from the fight though a few had started in on the Nazis at the back; grabbing at them and struggling to get their clubs away.

It was then she saw the gun…

"Suwan!" she screamed trying to push past Stubby, her eyes trained on the Nazi and his *Luger* aimed at Suwan's back. Kiri was struggling against a portly young man who strained his black shirt to its limits unaware of the danger she was in. "Suwan!" She shouted again her eyes widening in desperation and fear.

Suddenly there was another man in the fray. He was shorter and swarthy looking with his jet black hair. Obviously not with the Blackshirts but carrying a stick of his own, which came down hard on the gunman's wrist. He shouted something as the *Luger* went off firing twice into the pavement chewing up the stone cobbles of the plaza. Denise jumped and screamed at the gunshot then saw the gunman swing his arm back striking the interloper upside the head.

"Juden scum!" he spat as he leveled the gun at the other man.

The man pressed forward though even as the *Luger* exploded again. Denise saw the attacker plow into the Nazi then swing his fist in a roundhouse smashing into the German's mouth. More blood as the gunman staggered back with the force of the blow. She could see he was dazed, but still the gun came up again.

Kiri was there slamming the man's hand with the stick she had wrestled from her own assailant. The man screamed as limp fingers finally let loose on the pistol and it clattered away across the pavement and into the shuffling feet of the mob. She stepped forward slamming her palm into the gunman's other cheek and again Denise heard the sound of cracking bone. She knew Kiri, and this man had tried to kill so deserved no mercy.

Kiri stepped back crouching slightly then surged forward again driving her fingers into the stunned gunman's throat. He yowled, the scream turning into a gurgle as he stumbled back and away clutching at his neck. Denise had no idea what her friend had done but the Nazi was definitely crippled and no longer had the will to fight. Kiri let him run as she shoved at another man then swiftly knelt to scoop up the dropped gun. She popped the clip of bullets free from the handle then slipped both into the leather pouch she wore on her belt. And then she moved back into the fray.

"I'm outta film."

Denise blinked and turned to Stubby staring incredulously at his outburst. "What?" she asked as he held up his camera with a sheepish expression.

"I'm outta film, Miss Denise. I'm sorry."

Denise yelped as a hand fell on her shoulder. Without a thought she spun about, her own hours of pugilist training with her mother and simple self-defense with Suwan springing to the fore, taking over. Her hand curled into a fist ready to strike, swinging.

Suwan caught her fist in mid-punch; a slap of flesh on flesh. Denise gaped as her adrenaline spiked, the heat of the sudden riot threatening to sweep her up in the commotion. She worked her mouth trying to speak but nothing came out. Suwan's dark eyes seemed to bore into her.

"We should go," Kiri insisted in a cool tone. She nodded towards the Blackshirts and Denise saw the men gathering up their injured and shouldering their way through the crowd but away now, running.

"The police are at the edge of the mob," she continued with concern, "and the crowd is growing irritable. Things are about to turn violent."

Denise blinked again and turned to look where Suwan indicated. The police were pouring into the park from Sixteenth Street and further up from Park Avenue in force. Even from a distance Denise could see they were clubbing their way deeper into the mob using their nightsticks. Denise turned back to Suwan nodding and finally her friend released her fist.

"Hurry," Suwan urged and started shoving people aside clearing a path for the three of them towards the southern end of the park at Fourteenth Street. Denise grabbed hold of Stubby and started to follow when someone caught her eye. The man who had saved Suwan from being shot stood cradling his arms not so far away. She ran to him.

"Thank you," she cried then saw the blood on his suit. "You're hurt," Denise gasped grabbing at his hand to see the raggedy bullet hole. "Oh my god!"

"Shot," the man shrugged and winced forcing a smile, "It's nothing." He placed his hand back over the wound. "I have friends..." He turned and looked into the seething mass of people, Denise following his gaze. She saw no one rushing to his aid.

"Come with us," she urged grabbing his good arm. "We can help you. A doctor..."

"I don't..."

"C'mon! Stubby, help."

Denise started pulling the man after her as good ole' Stubby shoved from behind. Suwan was waiting impatiently until they caught up. The four of them then ran free of the thinning crowd even as the police paddy wagons roared up Fourteenth with sirens blaring. They ran for University Place, downtown and towards home at Washington Square Park just a few blocks away.

◉◉◉

"There we go."

Diane Pulitzer heard the loud 'clank' as Helga her housekeeper dropped the bloody bullet into the metal tin of water set nearby. She took a sip of her whiskey as the older woman wiped the man's wound clean, first with hot, soapy water and then alcohol before applying a wide, thick sterile bandage swathed in medicinal tape. Not the prettiest package she had ever seen but then Helga had learned her trade as a Field Nurse on the battlefields of the Great War. She got the job done; that's what counted.

"It was deep," Helga continued, wiping her hands on a towel then gathering her implements and dropping them into another dish filled with alcohol for cleaning. "Easier to cut it out of the back of the arm; it almost went all the way through." She shrugged. "I'm surprised it didn't. A *Luger* is a powerful handgun and at the range you say, well, you were very lucky."

"I dare say," Diane added as she plucked the bullet from the tin and rolled it around in the palm of her hand scrutinizing it. It looked like any other bullet she had seen over the years; a small slug of abused, overheated lead. "Another few inches to your left and the wound might have been worse; even fatal."

"You were very lucky, young man," Helga agreed with a wink and motherly tone as she stood picking up her serving tray with the dishes, towels and the tools of her trade. She took a final glance around. "You keep that clean and dry now and put no strain on it. See your doctor as soon as you can, within a day or two at least. He may want stitches." She looked to Diane. "If there's nothing else, Ma'am, I'll put these away and check on dinner. It will be a trifle late, I'm afraid." Diane Pulitzer smiled.

"Of course, Helga, and thank you."

"Yes, Helga. Thank you so much," Denise Pulitzer added from the roll top desk in the corner of the parlor where she was trying to sort her notes after the day's events.

"Thank you, Ma'am," the man finally spoke to Helga though he nodded at the entire group of assembled women. With a wide smile and blushing slightly from the praise Helga bustled out of the room off to the kitchen.

Diane strolled back to her chair and sat smoothing her skirt beneath her and crossing her legs at the ankles before holding up the bullet between thumb and forefinger examining it again. "I've fired a *Luger* before; a fine gun. German of course, manufactured first in the early 1900's, I believe. Daddy—my grandfather actually—has one in his small collection in his study upstairs." She rolled the bullet in her fingertips. ".30 caliber, I believe." Diane dropped the slug into a small glass dish on the end table with a 'tink'.

"It hurt," the man offered as he slipped back into his white shirt fingering the small hole in the sleeve and the blood stain with a frown. Helga had insisted on helping him strip down to his undershirt earlier the better to treat his wound. He winced slightly then as he sloughed into his thread-bare jacket. "I can shoot one but I'm afraid I don't know much about guns."

"Few people do," Diane explained. "My grandfather, Joseph Pulitzer, taught me how to shoot, and more importantly to know and respect fire-arms. I've tried to instill that knowledge and respect within my daughter, Denise, Mister…"

"Rosenfeld," the man offered again, "Matthew Rosenfeld."

"I'm sorry, Matthew," Diane apologized, "Thank you." Diane took a cigarette from the small wooden humidor on the table then offered one to their guest, which he took with a nod of thanks producing a lighter for them to share. After a long draw and some consideration he continued.

"I only saw the one gun. I'm sure there were others but does it really matter what make or model it was? Guns kill regardless, or rather people kill."

"In this case it might," Diane countered. "That these Nazi Blackshirts carried a German *Luger* might mean they are purists in their beliefs and ideals." She picked up a long baton, which she had set leaning on the table earlier. "And this; it's a truncheon, a *knüppel*." She held it up for everyone to see. It was long at over a foot made of polished black wood, thick and look-ing heavy. The handle was wrapped in fine dark leather with a long, looped strap to hold a proper grip. Denise could see odd symbols carved into the wood, though she didn't know what they meant.

"It looks like a billy club," Denise offered and Diane nodded.

"It does, but this one was custom made," Diane continued as she hefted the weapon. "It's well-balanced and by the weight I believe steel-shanked; nasty."

"It may be well-made," Suwan Shinobi spoke up from her place on the window seat cast in the final glow of the setting sun, "but the man wielding it was not skilled. I took it easily."

"Be that as it may," Diane went on, "this coupled with the *Luger* and how you described them I think means these Nazi sympathizers are quite serious."

"They're zealots," Rosenfeld offered as he took the truncheon inspecting it closer. He ran his fingers over the engravings. "We've encountered them before. They love their homeland as much as we do even though they are here in America and wish to bring their ideals, Hitler's ideals, with them. These runes carved into the wood signify the *Gestapo*—Hitler's secret

"Rosenfeld, Matthew Rosenfeld."

police; the *Schutzstaffel*." He smirked. "The youth carrying this weapon would be severely reprimanded I think if a true, ranking officer found him using this."

"The SS," Diane explained. "I've heard stories. You're German as well then?"

"I'm American!" Matthew exclaimed proudly then calmed, handing the weapon back to Diane. "I immigrated here legally through Ellis Island in 1935 with several of my friends, all believing—desiring—to start a new life in this 'Promised Land'. What we found was little better than what we left behind, however. Our ghetto here is only slightly better than what Warsaw has become and we encountered racism and bigotry at every turn." He paused, finishing his own whiskey and taking a long drag on his cigarette.

"I was born in Warsaw, so Polish in origin to answer your question, but my father moved our family to Munich in 1933 after Hitler became Chancellor and called for all those skilled to come forward and help in the recrafting of what would become his war-machine. My father was a machinist and back then—it wasn't so long ago I guess—Hitler did not care who worked in his factories. He only wanted results. The atrocities started after..."

The room was silent for some time as everyone thought on that. They had all seen the Newsreels in the theaters and rumors abounded of some of the things it was whispered the Nazis were doing to those they deemed not worthy or of pure German stock. The people of Jewish descent seemed to get the worst of it, Diane knew, herded off to ghettos and worse. The *Associated Press* had reported strange goings-on in Buchenwald about that, but nothing had been proven.

"My father, mother and younger sister were 'relocated' early in 1935; herded onto a train and sent away. I don't know where. I escaped that and tried to find them for a short time after, but by then Hitler's Shock Troops and soldiers were everywhere enforcing Nazi laws. So my friends and I fled here. We do what we can against those others, your Blackshirts, but no one listens or wants to help. The war will come here too, eventually, unless Hitler is stopped."

"I agree," Diane cut in, pouring another short whiskey for herself and Matthew. "I've said as much in my editorials for the *New York World* as well as broadcasts with *World News Radio*. Europe's war will come here sooner than we all might think. Hitler and his regime and *Reich* have only begun in their mad desires to change the world to their liking. They're racists and bullies plain and simple and hear nothing but their own jaded views and what they want to hear and everyone else is beneath their contempt. They won't listen and…"

"Diane." Suwan cut her off and rose from the window seat to place her hand on her friend's arm. Diane looked to her smiling friend then to her fist gripping the whiskey bottle by the neck with white knuckles. She took a deep breath and set the bottle down. She picked up her cigarette from the ash tray and took a long draw, blowing smoke to the ceiling before turning to Suwan again.

"I was ranting again?" Suwan nodded as Denise chimed in.

"Yes, mother," she laughed, "and it was going to be a lulu."

"I'm sorry," Diane apologized as she took her seat again setting the bottle aside. "It just makes me so angry."

"Don't apologize," Matthew offered, "Never apologize for your passion. I just wish more people shared your views rather than spouting their own narrow-minded opinions. The world needs to know, before it's too late. You have the power to spread the word with your newspaper and radio broadcasts, and you should every chance you get." Diane smiled swirling her whiskey in her tumbler as she considered the man.

"Who are you, Matthew Rosenfeld?" she finally asked. "You mentioned friends; who are they and where?" Diane thought for a moment. "What can we do to help your cause?"

It was Matthew's turn to consider as he took a long inhale on his cigarette. He looked to the three women in the parlor taking in each in turn; Diane who was the obvious matriarch of the house seated almost regally in her throne, Denise the daughter and heir apparent to the Pulitzer Empire, attentive on the edge of her seat as she listened, and Suwan Shinobi, quiet but always watching and ready to act. All three women helped him without reserve when he needed it most. He felt he could trust these women and this entire household—the Pulitzer Manse, rich but warm—with all his secrets. He downed his whiskey in one fiery gulp, crushed out his cigarette and sighed before he spoke.

"My friends and I follow the ideals of the *American Jewish Committee*… to a point. The AJC are good in what they do, and my people and their plight need a voice here in America to educate, but that voice is often too quiet. Sometimes actions speak louder than words and I've learned too the sword can sometimes be mightier than the pen.

"I am part of a smaller group as well," he went on waving off a refill of his crystalline tumbler. "My longtime friends and I, some others we've met here in America. We call ourselves the *Judean People's Front*." He gave a slight snort. "Somewhat pretentious I suppose, but we have high hopes and dreams of a better world and life without the dark shadow of Nazi prejudice." He saw Denise exchange a quick glance with Suwan at his words but did not know why.

Diane pursed her lips, tilting her head in thought. "I'm not overly religious, Matthew," she spoke after a moment, "but I believe that was an ancient land sacred to the Jewish people in Israel. Is that right?" Matthew nodded.

"Close enough," he agreed. "A tumultuous land throughout history, full of strife and hardships from famine to war; all four Horsemen have visited my ancestral homeland for that matter. The constant struggle in that land is why we chose our name. Not many here would understand its significance, but it fits with the struggle now and the rise of the Nazis and their atrocities. They must be stopped."

"You said you are Polish," Suwan spoke up and all eyes turned her way, "yet you name yourselves for a long dead land half a world away."

"My ancestors were born and lived for generations in the *Holy Land*. My great grandparents migrated to Poland in the 1800's to escape drought and hopefully build a better life for their children. They never forgot their heritage though and instilled that love and dedication of my people, religion and beliefs in me and my entire family. I'm proud to be Jewish, and no less so because of where I grew up or where I live.

"And not so different than you, I think, *samurai.*"

Suwan Shinobi was a bit taken aback by that, the passion in his voice and demeanor. She had found there were few here in America who even considered Japan, let alone who might know the history of her native land of *Nippon*. But Matthew Rosenfeld was correct in both their homelands were rife with turmoil over the centuries. Her own heritage seemed as confusing as his; born of a Japanese father and Chinese mother but raised by her grandfather and taught in the ancient arts of *Bushido*: the ways of the samurai. She sighed and nodded.

"I meant no disrespect. I fear I know less of your people and their history than you do of mine. I did not understand and merely wanted to learn." She saw the man relax and a slight smile crossed his lips.

"None taken," he waved her off as he lit another cigarette, relaxing again. "I've just encountered so much hatred here… I'm easy to set off. I apologize." Suwan nodded returning his smile.

"We're all friends here," Denise added looking on intently. "No need to get hot under the collar."

"There's not," Diane agreed draining her latest drink, setting the glass aside with a thump. "Enough of that," she mused shoving the bottle to the far edge of the table. She cocked her head again sniffing the air even as Helga poked her head through the door.

"Dinner's ready, Miss," Helga announced wringing her hands in her apron.

"Thank you, Helga," Diane acknowledged with a wide smile to the older woman. "It smells delicious as always." Helga beamed and backed out of the doorway.

"What say we move this discussion to the Dining Room, Matthew, where you can explain to us all what exactly we need to do to help."

Diane rose and returned the whiskey bottle to the liquor cart and continued on towards the kitchen. The others soon followed, the discussion over for now.

◎◎◎

Camp Siegfried
Yaphank, New York
Long Island

It's part of the *Amerikadeutscher Bund*, the German-American Bund movement called the *Friends of New Germany*," Rosenfeld explained as the group disembarked the Long Island Railroad train in Yaphank, Long Island. It was midday—the next day—and they could all feel the unseasonable warmth rising. It was May in New York and summer was already beating on the door. The frigid, icy winter of the past season would be followed by a hot, steaming summer it seemed.

Suwan Shinobi sniffed as she took in the surroundings, not impressed with the hamlet of Yaphank. The railroad station was little more than a shack set a few yards from the tracks; a platform with a waiting station and a sleepy guard and ticket agent in his office. Beyond was a small town with no buildings over three-stories; old shops and houses, churches and a strangely shaped schoolhouse. There was a lake off to the north, Upper Lake, Rosenfeld named it, and the camp, which was their ultimate destination though it was mostly hidden by the trees, out of sight. Suwan had accompanied Diane to several villages on Long Island in the past, but they were mainly on the North and South Shores; whaling towns and fishing hamlets. Yaphank was Middle Island, farmland and aside from the solitude Suwan could not see the attraction.

It had been a long ride to the hamlet, over three hours on the mainline train to Greenport, though Suwan had to admit it was much more comfortable than the trip she had taken from San Francisco years before. The old 'Iron Horse' was replaced by electric locomotives attached to battery-powered cars all energized by an electrified 'Third Rail', like the New York Subways. They caught the train in Manhattan's *Pennsylvania Station* traveling underground and then a portion of New York Harbor to change trains in Brooklyn's *Jamaica Station*. Then it was a straight ride through Queens deeper into Long Island proper through mostly flat, boring farm land stopping at the occasional towns, which grew smaller and smaller along the way.

"It was established some years ago," Rosenfeld told them again as they walked, "by a man named Fritz Kuhn and Heinz Spanknöbel to support National Socialism and the Third Reich after May 1933, though they have been recruiting since 1924 I believe. Deputy Führer, Rudolf Hess gave the *German National Socialist German Workers Party* permission to establish such camps in America and other sympathetic countries with German immigrants." Rosenfeld explained all this on the train ride earlier and the way it sounded Suwan thought he had probably explained it all before many times. He knew his facts.

"Except for a small faction, I would hardly say sympathetic, Matthew," Diane Pulitzer countered as they walked leisurely towards the lake in the distance and the camp. She shouldered her parasol against the sun trying to seem the lazy tourist come up from the City for a pleasurable day in quiet Long Island. "More apathetic I think."

"Unconcerned or uncaring is closer," Matthew offered kicking a small stone from the path as they strolled. "America is a brutal, segregated country, which ignores world events all too often for their own concerns. But for Roosevelt, our overworked leader, most people would not even know of the serpent in their midst, underfoot."

"Don't tread on me," Denise spoke up scribbling in her notepad, "that's great." Diane regretted allowing her daughter to come along at first, but Denise's enthusiasm won out in the end and she had to acknowledge she had in fact given her daughter the initial story to cover in Union Square. It was only right she saw it all the way through to the end, whatever that might be. Denise was taking snapshots with her Kodak camera as well and jotting down everything she heard. The story would hopefully be good.

"It holds true to the ideals of the Pro-Hitler group, the *Free Society of Teutonia*, and others. It draws hundreds every summer; advertising as a 'Summer Camp' get-away. Families come mostly from the City and the Boroughs, Upstate, Connecticut and New Jersey, though they have their fair share of similar places. I've visited some. But all the camps preach Hitler's teachings of a pure Germany and the Aryan race that should be in control."

"It's sickening," Suwan contributed as she peered through the windows of a Curios shop along the way. "But I've seen it before, in my homeland. The Empire recognizes the classes and segregates much the way your Germany does."

"It's not my Germany..." Matthew elucidated shoving his hands in his pockets. He looked bitter, Suwan thought. "Not anymore; now it belongs to the Nazis and their Third Reich." Matthew grew silent for a time as they walked along, the others following suit.

"It seems pleasant enough," Denise finally spoke, speaking of Yaphank, tired of the grim silence, "just another sleepy town out in the suburbs."

"It's a masque," Diane explained. "The Nazis are very good at hiding and disguising themselves, their intentions when they want to. The German people," she glanced at Rosenfeld, "and the Jews found that out too late." Rosenfeld nodded lighting a cigarette.

"It was not pleasant," he smiled at Denise, "in that time before I escaped. And it's getting worse."

"It always gets worse," Suwan admitted, her hand on the hilt of her *bokken* hidden beneath her light trenchcoat, "before it gets better."

Denise dashed up ahead of the group and just as suddenly turned bringing her camera up. Before any of them could protest she snapped a quick photo giggling all the while then turned and continued on at a quicker pace. Suwan could see they were nearing the camp and her enthusiasm over her story was clouding her judgement.

"Wait!" Rosenfeld called after her, but it was too late as Denise disappeared into the first cluster of trees edging on the lake. He started to hurry after her but Diane placed a hand on his arm to stay him. He turned to the publisher. "She should stay with us. There's danger..."

"I'm afraid Denise has the scent of the story," Diane mused with a smile. "I smell it myself, but it's her story," she shrugged, "and she'll be fine." Matthew still looked worried as Suwan gave her friend a sidelong glance, knowing better.

"I'll catch up to her," she offered and hurried on ahead before the others could protest. Suwan knew both women well, and their 'nose for news' quite often outweighed their better judgement.

Suwan could see the camp better in the distance now following a path off the main road from the town. It seemed a private community set away from Yaphank; a gathering of several small bungalows and suburban-type ranch houses with well-kept lawns, situated about Upper Lake. She could see people as well, youths as well as adults, men and women alike partaking of activities: an archery range, a swimming pool and the like, things to entertain. She could also see a staggered fence set up surrounding the 'private' community as Diane had named it, as well as an arching gateway proclaiming the camp's name: *Camp Siegfried*. There were also flags, which Suwan recognized.

The newsreels she had seen amidst the bizarre, animated cartoons and short movies showing before the main attraction on their many outings to the cinema often displayed world events. Among those were the troubles in Europe and the worsening threat of Nazi-ruled Germany. The newsreel films were tame showing flickering images of life in that far off land, but Suwan recognized the false trappings hiding what truly lay beneath. She had seen it all before in her native Nippon and *Edo*, Tokyo, when the samurai were driven into hiding, later out of existence. It was horrible and grand all at once with armies, banners and flags; unbelievable pageantry, which she saw echoed here in the camp. Echoes of the past she had lived through.

Raised voices in the copse of woods ahead drew her attention and Suwan immediately changed. She hunkered low and hurried at a brisk pace through the trees and shrubbery towards the lake following the noise. She heard Denise's voice rising in pitch and several others, male, sounding agitated, and almost threatening. Finally breaking through the scrub at the shore of Upper Lake she found Denise surrounded.

She saw a party of five young boys dressed in short-pants and long-sleeved, brown shirts adorned with ribbons, medals and pins, which shined reflecting the sunlight. All wore a red armband on their left arm proudly displaying the Nazi Swastika. They were part of the *Hitlerjugend*, the Hitler Youth, which Rosenfeld described on the train ride. They had surrounded Denise, accosting her with jibes in their language along with an older boy obviously in command. He was dressed more regally wearing long black pants and a matching black shirt equally adorned with regalia. A handsome lad in his late teens, blond and blue-eyed she could see from the distance and brandishing a black truncheon resembling the one Diane had shown them.

Suwan was moving even as one of the younger boys grabbed the strap of Denise's camera tugging at it, trying to snatch it away. Denise of course fought back, but they were children. Suwan learned long ago that did not matter. Children could be as cruel and merciless as adults, and often more so.

"Leave her alone," Suwan ordered as she burst into the small clearing. All eyes turned her way but no one moved as she expected. They were all caught up in the heat of the moment and she was hardly imposing, especially to the likes of them.

"Who are you?" the older boy turned towards Suwan wearing a smug, arrogant expression. He was perhaps eighteen, a swaggering youth in his domain.

"Let her go."

The children laughed some speaking German, others in English, not impressed with her by the gist. The older boy sneered and looked at Denise with contempt before turning to her again. "She is trespassing," he explained with an accent lacing his voice. "These lands," he gestured about him, "are privately owned by the German-American Settlement League. Your friend, I assume, should have stayed on the marked roads and trails."

"I didn't know," Denise offered in her own defense, bogus as it sounded. "I was just taking some snapshots." She smiled innocently, holding up her dangling camera still in the grip of one of the younger boys by the strap. "Keepsakes…"

"Lies!" he snapped snatching her purse before stepping towards Suwan. He dug through to her wallet and took it out thumbing through it with a smirk. Finally he paused and held up a small placard. Suwan recognized it even as he read.

"Denise *Pulitzer*," he spat her last name, "member of the *New York World*. That rag. I know the name, *Pulitzer… Jewish*. I might have known." He stuffed the wallet back into Denise's bag then tossed that at Suwan's feet. He spoke something in German at the boys and the one gripping Denise's camera strap jerked it free. He threw it to the ground then stomped down hard, smashing it.

"You will leave now," the older boy commanded Suwan. "She I will take to the Commandant."

"No," Suwan countered in a soft voice. "We are visitors here; guests. We'll both take our leave." The one in charge did not even turn but spoke to the others in a commanding German tone. Two of the boys grabbed Denise's arms and started trying to drag her away. Denise struggled but Suwan could tell she did not want to hurt children. Neither did she, but she would

"You will leave now!"

not allow her friend, her charge to be taken away. She moved towards the group not expecting trouble.

The older boy turned in a swift action raising his truncheon high and bringing it down in an overhand assault. Suwan shifted her stance and brought up her arms defensively. She blocked the attack with ease, sweeping his blow to the side. She stepped into him then followed through to cradle his arm within her own. She grabbed his wrist and pinched twisting in and making him squeal in pain. The truncheon fell from his hand landing in the grass as she held on thrusting upwards. A swift motion using his momentum against him she pulled down again. Off balance the boy lost his footing and she flipped him onto his back in the dirt. He huffed and shook his head.

"*Vas?*" he moaned wondering what had just happened.

Kiri surged forward and shoved the closest boy aside ignoring him as he stumbled and fell. She grabbed hold of the next, one who was holding Denise and pried his hand loose applying pressure to his thumb, twisting it back. He squeaked and let go until she set him free. She leaned past Denise and pushed her palm into the next boy's chest. He huffed and let go of her friend, staggering back to land on the ground.

"Go!" she told Denise but she stood frozen by the sudden activity.

"They're just little boys," she whispered.

"Bullies are bullies, Denise, no matter their age," Kiri replied stepping between her friend and the rest of the group. "Now go!"

"Halt!"

Kiri shifted her stance at the sound of the new, harsh voice on the scene. Three men were approaching all older than the oldest youth she just fought, older than she by their apparent appearance in fact. All three were dressed immaculately: two uniformed in pressed woolen military dress despite the heat with polished buttons, brocades and gleaming black jack-boots. The two outer men wore the more standard *Reichswehr* of a German soldier; earth-grey Jodhpur like pants and the longer, formfitting field-blouse sporting many pockets and a high, dark green collar bearing the *Litzen* insignia.

The man who had called out striding between the other two was obviously in charge, not only because of his older age, demeanor and swagger but the cut of his dress. His uniform was black with white and red trim about the underlying shirt, cuffs and pockets, with even more pomp and flash in the polished buttons and clasps. He wore two medals on his left breast, markings for his rank and bore a stylized eagle above a swastika on his left arm in place of the red armband. He wore black leather gloves and carried a 'swagger stick', like a riding crop, his high collar bearing jagged lightning bolts looking like 'S's. All three men wore holstered side arms and removed their visor caps, which sported the same Nazi eagle shifting them under their right arms as they came to a halt before Kiri and Denise.

The man in black looked to the fallen youth with disdain and disappointment. He glanced at those still on their feet with a mean sneer and Suwan got the feeling he was wondering why they were still standing. He shook his head and glanced at the man on his right who swiftly snapped to attention and barked out a command.

"*Beáchtung*!" he shouted and the others all moved to obey. The youngsters still on their feet drew to attention with immediate response. It took the other three a bit more time to get up but soon all were snapped to and appearing worried. The man in charge gave them all a final long look and sniff of contempt before taking another stride closer towards Kiri. Denise moved beside her and the man looked them both over, up and down finally turning to the younger Pulitzer.

"Who are you? Why are you here? This is private property." Denise was quick to respond whipping out her 'Press Pass'.

"Denise Pulitzer: *New York World*." Denise saw his obvious scorn as he examined her card.

"Ah," he sniffed, "a journalist. And just what are you doing here? Come to write another slanted fairy tale about the horrors of the Nationalist Regime in my homeland? Print another piece of *Yellow Journalism* denouncing the Third Reich?" Denise gave a slight gasp, bristling as she snapped her small leather sachet closed.

"I recognize your name, *Mädchen*. Your father... no, grandfather more likely was Joseph Pulitzer I suspect. I'm well aware of his private war with William Hearst in the last century; their sensationalism in the news stories they presented."

"I write what's important; news!" Denise snapped. "I'm here investigating your camp's involvement in the riot in Union Square on the First. I saw first-hand several members associated with your movement starting trouble and inciting violence. I'd like to hear what you have to say about that, and so would my readers." The man smirked looking thoughtful for a moment.

"Ah, yes," he mused, "the altercation at the annual working-man's rally. I heard about that. Obviously a simple discussion, which became overheated between opposing views in the moment of excitement." He shrugged.

"I've seen it before. It happens." He turned to face Suwan.

"And you, *Mädchen*?" Suwan glanced at the children still standing at attention then faced their inquisitor. She spoke before Denise could fill the silence.

"Suwan," she spoke simply, "a friend of Miss Pulitzer. And I am not a child." The man looked surprised.

"You speak German?" he asked.

"Jawohl, Herr Oberst."

"We all do, to some extent, and she's a friend of mine," Diane's voice exclaimed as she and Rosenfeld strode closer at a brisk pace hoping to quell the situation. "Diane Pulitzer, owner and editor of the *New York World*. I'm sure you've heard of me then as well." The man nodded looking over the new arrivals, his expression never flinching.

"I have," he acknowledged after a moment, "and it is an honor. Your journalism at least presents something closer to the entire picture and not the slanted views I've read in other, more questionable news sources." He pulled a small cigarette case from one of his many pockets and withdrew a cigarette then held out the case to Diane. She declined and he shrugged, shutting the case again with an audible snap, then secreting it away again before lighting his, ignoring the others. He glanced at Rosenfeld but did not address the man, the Jew.

"I heard there was an Oriental involved in the altercation in Union Square," he looked to Suwan, "one who 'incited' as well. Would that be you?"

"I was there," Suwan responded with the slightest nod of her head. "I was protecting Denise from your followers."

"And doing a remarkable job, I've heard." His smarmy smile chilled her. "Crowd control is an unforgiving occupation; I've done my share."

"And just who are you?" Diane took over the conversation again, stepping closer before Denise could say anything in defense. "By the adornment on your uniform, I gather, Colonel..." The man went to slight attention with a snap of his boot heels.

"Colonel Wilhelm Niedermaier," he proclaimed with no little pride. "I am *Kommandant* of this, *Camp Siegfried*. I must apologize for the overzealous actions of my charges. It reflects badly on them and our teachings here, and thus reflects badly on me."

"So why did they attack me?" Denise cut in. Niedermaier frowned then just as swift the smile was back in place.

"We have a rule prohibiting photography without written permission. There are forms to be filled out in our offices and protocols to follow. Had you entered through the main gate you would have been met and allowed with the proper papers. I assume you did not."

"We didn't know," Diane offered in apology.

"No real harm done," Niedermaier suggested looking at his youthful troops, "except perhaps a lesson in humility. If you would care to follow me, I'm certain we can correct the error."

"My camera's been smashed," Denise accused pointing a finger at one of the young boys, "That one." Niedermaier frowned turning towards the youth in question.

"He shall be happy to recompensate you, Miss, no worries. Please…" The *Kommandant* bowed slightly gesturing deeper into the camp with a flourish.

"Happily," Diane accepted for the group, but the Colonel paused.

"One moment, please." Niedermaier turned to the man standing back at his right. "*Stabsführer*! Put this squad on Report. Two weeks menial labor; kitchen detail and grounds maintenance, latrines. Then speak to the *Aufseher*… the overseers of the classes." He looked to Diane who nodded at the translation. "Inform them they are lacking in their teachings on how to welcome visitors."

"*Jawohl, Mein Oberst*!" the apparent deputy leader acknowledged. He immediately started shouting in German at the *Hitlerjugend*, who ran off just as swiftly as they could. Neidermaier watched until he was satisfied with their response, then turned back to the visitors. With another slight bow he gestured deeper into the camp.

"Please…"

◉◉◉

"Well, that was a load of…" Denise glanced at her mother who was watching her from the side, "garbage." Diane smiled.

"Yes, it was."

"*All* they have to say is 'garbage' as you call it," Rosenfeld agreed. "It was the same in Germany before I left. The Nazis speak to the masses inspiring them with a better way under their rule blaming the lesser races for the ills of the world; the poor conditions and poverty, lack of employment, the global economic Depression in general. To hear them speak of it, it was the Jews who caused the stock market crash in 1929 with their money-grubbing ways.

"Unfortunately when times are desperate people most often turn to the speaker with the loudest voice and the most eloquent speech. In the case of Germany there were over six million unemployed and living in the poorest conditions not seen since the 'Dark-Ages'. And there seemed no hope at all. In 1930 German Chancellor Hermann Müller resigned in impotency because his government could not find a viable solution to the calamity, which had befallen our land. His replacement, Heinrich Brüning proved just as ineffective though because he could not get the *Reichstag*—the German Parliament—to agree to his actions and policies. Finally, in desperation President Hindenburg used Article 48 of the *Weimar Constitution*, which gave him the power to govern freely and pass laws by his decree. This undermined democracy and weakened the power of the Reichstag, which did seem to help somewhat but with the state of the world then, and now it was not enough."

Rosenfeld lit two cigarettes from the pack he purchased in a small shop within *Pennsylvania Station* before their journey. He passed one to Diane and continued, gathering his thoughts as they walked back to the train station in Yaphank.

"Between 1930 and 1933 support for the extreme right-wing Nazis and the extreme left-wing Communists soared. They became the loudest voice speaking to the common populace; middle class shopkeepers and artisans, farmers and agricultural laborers who wanted a solution to their problems and a return to a better life. They expounded on the bloodline of the true Aryan race and the glories of the old Germany in the days of the Kingdom of Prussia." Rosenfeld shook his head in disbelief. "Unfortunately the people listened.

"Joseph Goebbels used propaganda as a weapon. He supported the ideals of Adolph Hitler from the beginning and praised the rising *Führer Cult*; those who believed the man to be Germany's savior, who would rescue the country from the grip of depression. He expounded on the Nazi's goal to create the *Volksgemeinschaft*, the People's Community; one German people with the true heritage, which would bring back those glories of old, making other religions and social classes less and less relevant.

"They scapegoated the Jews and other *lesser* races for all Germany's ills labeling us sub-human. We became threats to racial purity and the economic future of the country. Again the people listened and gained hope."

"Propaganda is a powerful weapon," Diane agreed taking a long draw on her cigarette. "Desperate people wanting hope will believe any lies, no matter how outlandish, anything to make their country great again." Rosenfeld nodded.

"Unfortunately for all his twisted racism, Hitler was an incredible public speaker with an extraordinary power to win people over and Goebbels' propaganda campaign was very effective bringing huge support for the Nazis. They targeted the Jews and other groups of society using different slogans and policies to win their support. By 1932 the Nazis and other like-minded parties were committed to the destruction of the ineffective Weimar Republic. Their voices held sway in the Reichstag with many workers turning to communism. However the real beneficiaries were the Nazis. It was a horrible time for my people, and when Hitler was declared Chancellor in 1933 it only became worse."

"It sounds dreadful," Denise agreed as she jotted down scribbled short hand in her note pad.

"It always is." All eyes turned to Suwan as she spoke up from the rear. She quickened her pace to catch up to the group having paused at the windows of the curio shop again. Diane eyed her then glanced at the store.

"Something catch your eye, Dear?"

"It's just a trinket. It's nothing."

"Nonsense, you were looking in there before. Show me."

Diane caught Suwan's arm and led her back to the windows peering at the display within. Denise and Matthew watched from a distance as they spoke, Suwan finally pointing at something within. Diane smiled and disappeared into the shop.

"I'm sorry," Denise offered in apology with a wan smile, "Mother dotes on Suwan at times. They're old friends." She grinned. "I suppose I do too."

"Perfectly fine," Matthew chuckled. "Friends are good and we all enjoy our novelties, *ja*?" Denise nodded in agreement, a slight blush to her cheeks.

A short time later the two women emerged from the shop, Suwan carrying a small package. Denise stared on curious but Suwan offered no explanation as the four took up their stroll to the train station again. She was about to ask when Rosenfeld cut in.

"You were about to say something before?" he asked, directing his question to Suwan. She twisted her lip in thought as though trying to remember. Matthew was certain however she knew exactly what he was talking about.

"You were all speaking of the Nazis rise to power," she began, "and I was merely agreeing. It was somewhat the same in my native Nippon in the last century." Rosenfeld paused a moment to crush out his cigarette on the sole of his shoe. He dropped the butt into a small trash receptacle and hurried to where the women were waiting.

"I apologize. And I'm afraid I'm not as much a student of Japanese history as I am, well, knowledgeable at least of Germany's past." Suwan nodded, pursing her lips in thought.

"In the mid-1800's the West arrived in number to convince the young Emperor of Nippon, Kōmei, into greater trade with their countries. The Americans were the driving force, of course, but the English, French and various Spanish territories were involved as well. They were all quite convincing in their use of your propaganda in convincing the Emperor to abandon Japan's more isolationist ideals and join the rest of the world, opening its borders. The samurai at the time were not as enthusiastic about the change to their lifestyles as the rest of the country as well as the *Shogunate*. They still followed the Emperor's rule, as they had for centuries.

"The last true showing of the samurai was in the Boshin War when they defeated the shogunate forces in favor of the Emperor Meiji. But the last of the old samurai and *daimyōs*, the Lords and land holders, were abolished slowly after that and absorbed into the new Empire of Japan. It was a bloody time."

"You speak as one who lived through those times," Rosenfeld offered. "Surely you're not that old? I'm sorry..." he blushed, "one should never inquire as to a woman's age."

"My grandfather was my *sensei* and taught me many things after my parents died." Suwan grew silent after that. Her part in the conversation was over.

"If everyone's satisfied then I think we should move on to our next step," Diane proposed as they arrived at the Long Island Railroad station platform Just as a horn blared in the distance, "which I suppose would be getting on the train and riding back to Manhattan. Here comes the train." She pointed towards the plume of smoke pouring up above the tree line in the distance.

"And what then, Mother?" Denise asked looking at the group. It was Rosenfeld who finally spoke.

"I think perhaps a visit to my world."

◎◎◎

Rivington Street
The Lower East Side
New York City

Matthew Rosenfeld weaved his way through the crowd glancing back every few seconds to make certain his charges were still close by and following along. Checking back over his shoulder he saw Diane Pulitzer pushing through the growing throng of onlookers gathered for the night's speaking event like she belonged. Her old journalist's training he assumed, trying to get to the heart of the story no matter what she came up against. She flashed him a smile nodding she was still there and fine.

Close behind Diane he saw her daughter Denise with her new *Leica* instant camera out as she snapped photographs of the crowd. Colonel Niedermaier had been true to his word in compensating Denise for her smashed camera. She seemed as determined as her mother as they moved closer towards the the back end of the hall where the speakers would hold stage, asking names and questions, wanting quotes and sources for her story. Rosenfeld knew both women would give a fair and honest account of the day's events no matter what might happen, which was good. He had spent some time last night reading a few of the elder Pulitzer's editorials as well as some past news articles, and though Denise only had one true byline to her name her writing was hard-hitting and to the point. He had no worries and it felt good to have someone as esteemed and respected as the Pulitzers on the side of his people at last. Perhaps now the truth and the horrors in Europe would come to light and be exposed.

Finally bringing up the rear and in the background as seemed to be her way was the mysterious Oriental woman, Suwan Shinobi. She was a strange one, quiet and reserved most of the time, but she voiced her opinions in no uncertain terms when she had some ideal to express. He liked that, even respected it; a woman who was outspoken and equal when needed. And she was willing to fight for her convictions and more importantly, for what was right. A truly remarkable young woman.

And now though she seemed to walk casually through the assembly he could see she was watching everything. Her face seemed almost serene but he noticed her dark eyes flitting about taking in the scene occasionally turning her head towards heated words or abrupt movement. She seemed to be scanning the gathering looking at faces and judging mannerisms, never straying far behind her friends, remaining within striking distance to protect the women she loved. Was she expecting violence today? If so he was certain she would be ready for it. He had seen firsthand in Union Square Park how she dealt with fools and bullies and he was certain she was prepared to do the same here should the need arise.

But, truthfully Rosenfeld was expecting violence as well, or at least loud, heated words. His friends were vocal in expressing their views and their hatred of what Germany had become. They were not who he was worried about however. The Nazis and their American *Bund* supporters were present in Union Square Park and other rallies held in New York and New Jersey over the last few months, whether the theme was labor, equality for all or his own Jewish people and their plight.

Activity on the stage drew his attention as they came closer. A portly, balding man was speaking on future activities in the New York area; scheduled rallies and upcoming protests to be held over the upcoming summer months. There were many, one a week almost, and sometimes two, all arranged in hopes of unifying his people and their cause. And there were others on the speaker's platform awaiting their turn. The day's rally was to be an all-day affair with many wishing to be heard. A few scurried about tending to the sound equipment and the lighting fixtures to be used throughout. A flurry of activity no matter what direction one looked.

"Who is that?"

Rosenfeld turned at Diane Pulitzer's voice, she suddenly at his side pointing towards the stage. By her inquisitive expression he knew he had been a negligent host. He smiled sheepishly.

"Sorry. That's Rabbi Stephen Samuel Wise, one of my friends, actually, that I wanted you to hear. He's a strong leader and a driving force in establishing the People as a unified front helping to create the *Federation of American Zionists* as well as the *American Jewish Congress*." Diane looked thoughtful for a moment, then spoke up over a wave of applause and cheers.

"I've heard of him. He was instrumental in forming a Jewish boycott of German goods some months ago, and just last year helped others organize the *World Jewish Congress* in order to better fight Nazism. 'The time for prudence and caution is past. We must speak up like men,'" Diane quoted and Rosenfeld stared at her with new respect. Diane shrugged.

"I read his speech; truly inspiring."

"A great man," Rosenfeld agreed brushing hair from his eyes. "His words are uniting Jews the world over as we learn more and more of the atrocities in Europe, whether fact or rumors. We need more like him."

Another roar of applause and cheers drowned out their conversation and Diane looked to the speaker's platform to see Wise waving to the audience with the Master of Ceremonies for the event at his side urging them on. Diane could feel the excitement in the tightly packed, smoke-filled room as well as the tension. As with any rally attended, no matter the subject, there were two sides present and as she scanned the crowd she could see those who did not share in Wise's enthusiasm, or the movement. Grim, dour men and women mingled within the audience; frowning and grum-

"That's Rabbi Stephen Samuel Wise."

bling with hatred smoldering in their eyes. Businessmen she imagined losing money because of the boycotts or possibly simply German immigrants remembering their homeland from a time before the Great War and now Hitler's rise. There were many German-Americans who were expatriates with no ties to the Bund. At times it was all too easy to forget that.

"Hey!" A shrill cry and bright flash of light drew Diane's attention back to the stage. There was her daughter, Denise holding tightly to her camera's strap again struggling with a man who seemed intent on ripping it from her grip. He was shouting at her and had the advantage being taller and appearing bigger as her daughter was almost petite but she was fighting fiercely, a trait shared by both Pulitzer women. Diane started moving forward with Rosenfeld at her side as the man reared back and slugged Denise squarely on the cheek.

"*Jüdische Schlampe!*" he shouted as Denise staggered back losing her grip on the leather strap. She stumbled against the stage even as the man pulled open her camera ripping out the long thread of film exposing it. The people standing near were backing away from the altercation while some in the audience rushed forward to help; but help who?

"Calm down!" the MC urged over the Public Address grabbing the microphone. Others on stage seemed stunned staring in confusion. The man threw the camera to the floor and Diane heard it shatter on impact even as he dipped his hand into his longcoat producing a short, metal tire iron. He brandished it high.

"*Umkommen!*" he raged.

And suddenly, Kiri was there…

◎◎◎

Without hesitation Suwan Shinobi stepped between Denise Pulitzer and the man. She grabbed his forearm high overhead and stepped in pulling it back and down. He arched backwards with a shocked expression on his face at her effrontery but she was not cowed by his bluster and boisterousness. She shifted her weight and stance bringing him back and flipping him over her thigh to land sprawled on the hardwood floor, the tire iron clattering away and out of reach.

Kiri gave Denise a quick glance and saw her young friend recovering, rubbing her injured cheek as she pushed back off the stage staring at the smashed camera. She sensed Diane and Rosenfeld shoving closer but they were not a concern. The man on the ground was shaking his head trying to

regain his senses while others—his companions she assumed—were raising voice in the crowd turning mob.

"You!"

Kiri turned back to the man she had felled, his face turned up at her,
accusing. She recognized that face though the man was clothed differently.
He was wearing a common, working man's clothes and like most in the
room, an overcoat against the cold. But he was the *Stabsführer*, the younger
deputy führer from their journey to *Camp Siegfried* on Long Island. She
knew now why Denise had singled him out for a photograph. His face was
twisted in rage.

"You are that *östlich schlampe* who accosted me and my men; made us
look fools with your eastern trickery," he snarled, struggling to his knees,
one hand slipped within the folds of his coat withdrawing a bottle and a
Zippo lighter, which quickly flicked afire.

"Never again; *der Angriff*!" he shouted throwing it.

The beer bottle tumbled through the air overhead, aflame. Kiri recognized it for what it must be; the bottle stuffed with a burning cloth. The *Mo-
lotov cocktail* hit the wooden floorboards of the stage with a fiery crash even
as she dove forward, tackling Denise and driving her to the floor. Denise
screamed as fire erupted blowing across the stage and out over the crowd.

More screams of terror and pain as Kiri looked down at her charge. Denise was wide-eyed more with shock than terror as people near the stage
panicked, some alight with fire dancing and burning their clothes and hair,
their bodies as they fought the press of the mob trying to get away.

"Are you all right?" she asked as Denise focused on her, her huge green
eyes clearing. She nodded trying to find words as another fiery explosion
drew Kiri's attention back to the stage; another bursting cocktail.

Men were beating at the raging conflagration with their overcoats but
doing little to contain it. Whatever the bottles had been filled with had been
highly flammable and spread on impact. She saw several of the speakers
dropping to the ground and rolling to extinguish themselves. The announcer
lay sprawled hanging half off the platform, his body burning and unmoving.

"*Jetzt stirbst du!*"

The deputy führer stood over her his face lit garishly by the raging fires
as his outstretched, shaking arm tried to steady the *Luger* aimed at her face.
His visage remained a masque of anger as he snarled.

"You have shamed me in the eyes of *mein Oberst* and *mein Führer*. I and
my comrades have been charged with the task to right that wrong." He
looked to the stage and then out to the panicking crowd. Most were push-

ing their way to the exits as the hall burned though a few were fighting the fire. Kiri heard sirens in the distance.

"The Rabbi has run like the *der Köter* he is," he sniffed, "but all the better to find you here. You and your *Jüdische mischlingsfreunde.*" Kiri brought up her hands even as his finger twitched at the trigger.

"No!"

Someone flew overhead shouting even as the gun fired exploding in a blinding flash and deafening noise. Rosenfeld had leapt at the youth trying to bull him away and down. Kiri saw his body jerk though as the struggling pair crashed to the floor. Still Rosenfeld wrestled with the teen, screaming as the gun went off again in a spray of blood.

"Get up!"

Kiri felt Diane grabbing at her arm trying to pull her to her feet. She shrugged off Diane's grip and rolled off Denise before springing up. She spun drawing her wooden *bokken* from her heavy winter overcoat. She whipped it high over her head parallel to the ground assuming the stance of *Kama*; ready to attack or defend.

The youth shoved Rosenfeld off him, spitting as the man rolled onto his back. Kiri saw blood at Rosenfeld's stomach and soaking the front of his shirt.

"*Jüdische abscaum!*" the youth cursed sneering at Rosenfeld. He turned to Kiri raising his gun again.

Kiri stepped forward, her sword sweeping down in a fluid arch. Her bokken slapped at the Hitler youth's hand knocking it away as the *Luger* went off. She felt a bullet tug at her coat as the gun tumbled up onto the stage, her sword whipping up again as she altered her grip. She clutched the hilt fiercely with both hands feeling her own anger boiling over. She stabbed down with all the force she could muster, her form and training forgotten as her vision filled with crimson rage. She heard a choked scream as she struck but ignored it as she stepped over the *Hitlerjugend* twisting her sword with a final shout of triumph.

"*Hai!*"

Breathing hard as the fury started to ebb she stared down at the young man; the misguided youth filled with anger and bigotry. Her boken stood driven deep into the youth's gaping mouth as he quivered in dying, eyes wide and rolling in disbelief. She watched him for a moment and felt no regret as she pulled her sword free. She knelt down and wiped her boken clean on his overcoat, staring as he gasped.

"*Du bist durch, Junge,*" she declared in German as she stood again. Blood soaked spittle and foam oozed from his mouth as he coughed and finally lay still. Her lips twisted in revulsion as she sniffed. "*Erledigt… * Done."

Diane was at her side again suddenly pulling on her arm. "We've got to get out of here," she shouted over the screaming crowd. Kiri saw the doors were clogged with everyone pushing and shouting. Some men brandished makeshift weapons striking out in every direction; the *Bund* she assumed, their cause forgotten in the panic of survival. Kiri nodded.

"Help me!"

She and Diane both looked to the source of the voice. Denise was kneeling at Rosenfeld's side pressing a bloody rag to the wound in his stomach. She was white with fright as she stared up at them, imploring.

"I can't stop the bleeding," she yelled over the din. Something on the stage exploded in a fiery burst; equipment burning hot. "He needs help! We have to get him out of here."

Diane was down beside them immediately scooping under his limp shoulders. She heaved as Denise tugged on Matthew's arm trying to help lift him.

"Take his legs," she ordered and Kiri bent to hoist his legs. Together the three women hefted him up and looked about for a way out of the hall.

"There!" Denise pointed at the nearest exit. The crowd was thinning and streaming through the doorway but Kiri saw one of the boys from Camp Siegfried wielding a truncheon at those about him as he fought for the door.

Still they started carrying Rosenfeld's form towards the portal. Alive or dead, Kiri could not tell, but the man had saved her there at the end. She had to try to save him at least. She had *giri* with him now; a debt she owed and would do all within her power to help him live.

"Here, Denise," she urged motioning for the younger Pulitzer to take the man's legs. Denise complied still looking frantic as they neared the exit and the boy with the truncheon. Fire licked at the walls of the old building, the rotted wood lighting and burning easily, casting the boy scarlet in its elemental fury. His face was twisted in rage like the others but there was also a glee in his visage as he battered the scared people trying to get past him. He was striking blindly at anything that moved with no remorse and a fervor of hatred. Kiri scowled as she pushed her own anger back down again.

She surged forward striking the boy's wrist and slid the wooden blade down at an angle. The truncheon fell free and clanked away in the confusion of panic. Without a thought to his youthful age she shifted and brought her elbow up to smash into his nose. The boy flew back in a gush of blood to collapse on the hardwood floor. With a sigh she sheathed her blade and hefted him up upon her shoulders. She would not let a child die, misguided as he was.

"Suwan! C'mon!" Diane shouted as she and Denise carried their burden through the doorway. Denise looked at her with a panicked expression but kept moving until they all vanished through the portal into the flickering shadows beyond.

Kiri hefted the boy higher onto her shoulders and followed…

◉◉◉

New York-Presbyterian Lower Manhattan Hospital
170 William Street
Manhattan

Diane Pulitzer stubbed out her latest cigarette into the overflowing tin ashtray as the doors to the Emergency Ward shoved open. Denise shot to her feet from the hard wooden bench and hurried forward as the man who came through the doorway entered the semi-sterile corridor with a clipboard in hand. Suwan simply turned at his approach not moving from the spot she had chosen to stand stoically awaiting news of Rosenfeld's fate.

The man was older with thinning gray hair and a grim countenance, looking to the three women and some motion of hospital staff further down the hall. He was dressed in pale grays; baggy scrubs and wearing a blood-smeared apron and rubber gloves, cloth cap in hand. A mask dangled under his chin equally stained.

"How's Matthew?" Denise asked now standing before the doctor. The man looked to her, then at the papers on his battered clipboard and finally at Diane, the eldest of the three women.

"You're family?" he asked with a frown shuffling his papers.

"No," Diane answered rising as well. "We're the ones who brought Matthew in." The doctor frowned turning back through the sheaf of paperwork to the first page and finally nodded.

"Matthew Rosenfeld… Yes." He sighed and lowered the clipboard to his side. Finally he let a slight smile curl his lips.

"He'll live," he stated with assurity and all three women let out a breath of relief. "By the grace of God or sheer luck I don't even want to wager. The bullet in his stomach was superficial," he continued, "passed right through. The wound in his midsection should have normally killed him, but remarkably, or maybe amazingly that bullet missed everything important;

his inner stomach, his spine, kidneys. Nothing crucial was harmed. It was a stomach wound, technically speaking for the report, which accounted for all the blood, but again God must have stepped in or maybe his angel deflected the bullet." The doctor grinned looking to the Crucifix adorning the wall with reverence for just a moment.

"I got that one out with little fuss," he added. "I noticed another wound; another bullet?"

"Yes," Diane answered, "from a few days ago. My housekeeper was a nurse in the Great War, and she removed it. Again with little fuss." The doctor nodded.

"I'm Doctor Haskell by the way." He did not offer to shake hands.

"What of the others?" Suwan asked finally stepping up to join the group.

"Only two deaths, thankfully," Haskell offered, his face dour again. "William Rutherford? And a Hans Werner? He died of questionable circumstances. His carotid artery was severed."

"Rutherford was the Master of Ceremonies at the rally," Diane answered remembering the body hanging at the edge of the stage.

"He was dead on arrival," the doctor explained as he checked his notes. "Burned worse than anyone brought in; caught in the brunt of the blast I imagine. The rest have mainly burn injuries and smoke inhalation. Several in fact will be healing for quite a while, I'd say and probably needing therapy for some time to come. In all though with the fire and the crowd in attendance, well… Everyone was very lucky."

Suwan whispered bowing her head in prayer to *Yakushi Nyorai*, the Buddha representing healing and medicine. Awakening, peace and nirvana seemed most appropriate.

"When can we see Matthew?" Denise asked chewing her lower lip. Despite the doctor's good news she still seemed nervous and worried. Doctor Haskell shook his head.

"It'll be several days, I'm afraid. The bullet missed his lungs but he's still having some trouble breathing. He'll be in an oxygen tent until he seems more stable. Leave a name and phone number—if you have one—with the Ward Matron. You'll be called with any changes." He lowered his clipboard again.

"I'm afraid that's all I've got at the moment." He shrugged. "I should get back in there. They need help."

"Of course, Doctor," Diane offered, "and thank you for all your help." That slight smile again.

"That's why we're here," he stated with a final nod to the three women before turning and disappearing back through the doors and into the Emergency Ward.

Diane eventually went back to the long bench and picked up her cigarettes, sparking one to life. There were others sitting in the long corridor, all worried faces as they awaited news of their own friends and loved ones. They all went back to their own thoughts as the doctor took his leave awaiting the long wait for news of their own. She also noted two police officers at the far end of the hall questioning people.

"We should go now," she stated as she sloughed into her coat and gathered her bag. "There's nothing more to be done until we hear from the hospital. I'll telephone tomorrow though."

"Yes," Suwan agreed, but Denise hesitated still looking after the doctor and the Emergency Room doors. Nothing changed as the swinging doors finally stopped their motion. Denise turned and looked at the others down the hall and finally to her mother and friend.

"I just feel so damn helpless… Useless."

"You must have faith, Denise," Suwan professed holding up the younger Pulitzer's overcoat. Denise stared blankly at the garment for a moment then slipped her arms into the sleeves.

"Remember Ben Marino," she added, "and the docks." Denise remembered.

Ben Marino was her mentor at the *World*; an Ace reporter and the man who steered her on the proper course in her journalism. He had taken a spear near his heart, one probably meant for her, saving her life that night on the West Side Hudson Docks when Kiri had killed so many and faced her demon, Kareta Hana. It was a memory etched forever in her mind; Ben gasping for life, bleeding. He had survived but it had taken time and now, months later he still felt the pain. He probably always would.

But he survived, and Matthew would as well.

Denise smiled at Suwan as the tears flowed freely. She fell into Suwan's arms and hugged her with all the strength and love she could muster. Suwan Shinobi hesitated only a moment before wrapping her own arms tightly about her young friend, returning the embrace.

After some time Diane crushed out her cigarette in the tray, scooped up her daughter's purse and shouldered it with her own.

"Let's go home," she proposed, and it was so…

THE END

KIRI: RISE OF THE BUND ESSAY

I've always been a fan of comic books since the 60s. From there I learned of the old Pulps; the likes of the Shadow and the Phantom, Doc Savage, and so many more, and of course back then we had Batman and The Green Hornet on television, which only added fuel to my creative fires. Too, I am a role-play gamer from way back in the late 70's, making up characters and telling stories on the fly. All of that subtly molded me into the person and author I am today.

I wanted to be part of that culture, to be a cartoonist drawing comics initially, but that unfortunately did not pan out. So I turned my attention and focus to writing rather than drawing. With the advent of the Internet I found an outlet for my creativity, and eventually a website to post the first of my stories. That website was called Restrained Tastes, and the story was Kiri: Night of the Mist.

Kiri was actually my first heroine to find acclaim on the Internet, and her original story is the longest I have ever written, now easily passing 500,000 words and still ongoing. At the time I did not consider her to be a 'Pulp' character, but those who read that original piece said she definitely was and I had no problem with that, though that was not the initial intention for the character.

The website Restrained Tastes featured stories, articles and images all dealing with escapology, or more directly, Female Escapology. It was there in the site's Chat Room I first met the Webmaster and several very talented writers, all of whom encouraged me to give writing for the Site a go. I readily agreed and set out to do just that, though I wanted to do something a bit different.

Another passion of mine since moving to New York was the fascination of old Manhattan and how the city came to be. I love the old photographs and reading about the history of the city and figured that I could work that somehow into my story as well. Having plenty of inspiration and hard facts in books, role-playing game source books and the Internet—though this was before Wikipedia, I thought long and hard as to what to write, what character would serve. And it just came to me!

There was no pay involved in Fan Fiction, thankfully because I broke copyright infringement laws right and left. That original story became an episodic endeavor starring some of fiction's greatest characters: Doctors

Moreau and Jeckyl, as well as the insidious Fu Manchu. Set in the turn of the 20th Century Manhattan, each writing installment ended with Kiri and/or her confidant Diane Pulitzer bound, gagged and in some type of peril, much like the serials of the old 40's movies. Kiri herself was a Ronin Samurai, hunting the villain that slew her grandfather, master and sensei years before, along with her entire dojo, chasing the beast from Feudal Japan to America. I actually have a Western tale with her in old time San Francisco, part of her journey cross country, that has never seen virtual print.

Restrained Tastes has unfortunately closed, so that original story sits remarkably on my Hard Drive (after 30+ years and several computer crashes), though as you have hopefully just read, Kiri has been given life again. Through the help of Derrick Ferguson of Dillon fame, I submitted a story sample to Ron Fortier at Airship 27, which he liked but I had to work on. In the interim he suggested I write a short story for one of his titles: MYSTERY MEN (and WOMEN) Vol. 3, and of course I jumped at the chance to give Kiri a new home.

Which brings us to my latest story for Airship 27; Kiri: Rise of the Bund. This tale is actually not part of Kiri's original tale; it was in fact suggested by Ron Fortier himself. Ron asked me to write a story involving Kiri in New York battling Nazi saboteurs and having support from German immigrants who wanted nothing to do with Hitler and his 3rd Reich, but were being shunned by other New Yorkers for their ancestry. Well, my brain immediately started churning and soon came up with the threads of a story.

As stated above I was a New Yorker and had researched much of its past both for my stories and the pleasure of it. I knew of New York's involvement, during and after World War II and I had learned about the Nazi-sympathizing Bund as well as the camps created across the United States for German nationalists and sympathizers. I also learned of the Jewish plight in America; the racism and violence often directed at them. I had heard of it all, but I needed more.

Kiri: Rise of the Bund took a lot of research. I wanted to get my facts straight, and again I am thankful for Wikipedia and the Internet as most of my New York research books were donated to charity in my last relocation back to Oregon. Via the Internet I found websites that gave me all the information I needed; the Bund, the Hitler Youth movement, the Jewish community in New York and places and names. I had the character, the setting, the plot and ending. I was ready to write. The rest was easy. The 1st draft was finished within a couple days and the final version, which you hopefully just read was done within the week. Hope you enjoyed it.

I have many more stories in mind for Kiri, the Mist, which will hopefully see print; new ideas and old ones reworked, but regardless, as long as you enjoyed this one, I am happy. I am a storyteller after all, and I am here to entertain.

◎◎◎

CURTIS FERNLUND - was born May 15th, 1962 in Medford, Oregon, which is just a few miles north of the California border where he grew up with his parents and sister. He was raised there and went to school, worked and played until 1984 when he loaded up a U-Haul with most of his worldly belongings and drove cross country with three of his friends, eventually settling in Brooklyn, New York. A few years later he met his soul mate, Erica, and moved to Manhattan to live with her where they spent eighteen wonderful years together until her passing in 2006.

Arriving in Manhattan, he was hoping to get a career in the comic book industry as an artist, and though he did get some work published on occasion elsewhere he could not break into that field. He turned his focus to writing then, and that in Fan Fiction on the still developing Internet, as he had always been a comic book fan as well as of the older Pulp genre and a role-play gamer. After dozens, if not hundreds of stories posted on the Internet, another life goal was achieved, and he became a published paid author, thanks to Ron Fortier, Airship 27 and Erica, who always had faith in him.

Now over three decades later, older and hopefully wiser he's back living in Oregon, doing the best he can and of course, writing.

To read more of his work, go to Airship 27 (airship27hangar.com):
Kiri: Night of the Mist in *Mystery Men (& Women)* Volume 3
Kiri: Flight of the Valkyr in *Mystery Men (& Women)* Volume 6
The Queen of Escapes

PIMPIN' YOUR SUPERCAR
A DR. FIXIT TALE

By Greg Hatcher

Christine Vance glared at the floor nurse. "But he *knows* me. I've been here before."

"Doesn't matter." The nurse was stolid and expressionless, a thickly-built woman in her mid-fifties. She looked as immovable as Gibraltar. "Mr. Voskovec was very specific. No room for doubt. No visitors." She tapped a red laminated sign hanging from the doorknob to Ernie Voskovec's room with the words PRIVACY PROTOCOL printed on it in black letters.

Christine noticed the door was ajar. She leaned to the side and raised her voice. "Ernie! It's Christine! Are you up and around?" The floor nurse glared and opened her mouth to speak but before any words came out Christine added, "I brought doughnuts!"

"Doughnuts? Hot damn." The door swung open and there was Ernie Voskovec beaming at her from his wheelchair. He looked up at the nurse and said in an apologetic tone, "I'm sorry, Flo. I shoulda given you a list of okay folks. I just never get real visitors, usually, and I didn't want any reporters." His eyes twinkled and his seamed walnut-brown face split in a big smile. "Also? Anybody with pastry, you send 'em straight in. Even that asshole Gerry Baylor from the *Star*." The nurse nodded and moved to make a note on her clipboard and Voskovec paled. "No, I'm kidding, never let Baylor in here, I don't care if he's got prime rib." He turned to face Christine and added ruefully, "Him and that other guy, whatshisface, Heston over at *Newstime,* they're the reason I asked 'em to put the sign up. Those guys are getting on my last goddamn nerve. Anyway, c'mon in, toots." He pivoted his wheelchair with surprisingly easy grace, adding over his shoulder to the nurse, "You can put Chrissy here on the good list though, no press guys is what I meant. She's okay."

"Already done."

"Thanks." Voskovec turned back toward the room and wheeled himself in.

The nurse glanced at Christine, still expressionless, but somehow no longer hostile. "Vance? V-A-N-C-E?"

"Yes ma'am." Christine smiled brilliantly at her, trying to keep the gloat out of it. *No need to antagonize her; if Ernie agrees to my proposal I'll be spending a lot of time here.* She stepped into the room.

Ernie was over by the window, gazing out over the rest home's courtyard. He looked a little annoyed and Christine was apprehensive. "What are you looking at, Ernie?"

"Saw somebody out by the hedge. You being here made me wonder if Baylor was going to take another swing at it but it's just that idiot Merkel who's over in the other wing across from mine." At her blank expression he added, "He's trying to sneak a smoke. I don't know how he gets 'em in over there, they're all on staff watch, that's what 'skilled nursing' means. It's code for 'can't be trusted alone.' They get pretty strict here about stuff like that, the whole place went nonsmoking a couple months ago." He sighed. "I don't care about that but man, I miss having a cold beer in the afternoon. They don't let us have nothing. Flo was giving you the stinkeye and all you brought was doughnuts. That's practically contraband here." Abruptly Voskovec wheeled around to face her as though making a deliberate effort to shake off his pensive mood. He grinned. "Where are they, anyway? Give."

Christine smiled, relieved to see him in good spirits again. She handed him a small white bag. "I didn't know what you like so I brought an assortment." She paused. "I'm press too, you know, Ernie."

"I know. National Radio or whatever—"

"National Public Radio. NPR."

"Yeah, that." Ernie raised a roguish eyebrow. "But you're easy on the eyes, kid. Baylor's got a face like an overcooked potato and a voice only another foghorn could love. Sweet young thing like you, though..." Christine flushed and Ernie's grin softened. "Naw, I'm just funning with you, toots. You blush so easy; it makes it hard not to tease you a little." He grew serious. "No, really, I was just happy to see you so I could say thanks. I listened to that thing you did about me and Justin. You didn't use our names. You could have. I mean, I knew you was taping, I know how radio works."

"I just... it wasn't that kind of story." She shook her head. "The story was what really happened back then with Captain Dynamo and Diamond Brain and the battle of Easter Sunday, and that's where I tried to keep it. People want to know about the old St. Jacques supers and what that life was like. Masks and costumes and battles on the streets and all of that. So that's what I gave them. Anyway, you're a source," she finished. "I don't reveal sources. I'm kind of surprised anyone found you at all. I didn't even tell my boss who Dr. Fixit was. I don't know how the *Star* or *Newstime* got hold of it."

"I know it wasn't you. You'd have done it on the radio already if you was gonna do it. Naw, I think it was one of the night guys here, recognized my voice from the piece you did and tried to peddle it to somebody. Probably that punk that does such a shitty job mopping, that's got the headphones on all the time." He shrugged. "Doesn't matter. I don't talk to them report-ers, they can't do nothing. Everybody else who knew the real story is dead—other'n you and me. I just get sick of them bugging me about it." He grinned at her and raised his eyebrow again, this time with a wry expression. "But that journalist source stuff ain't why you did it. You didn't just find me, you found Captain goddamn *Dynamo*. That's Pulitzer territory, you know it is. They been after him for years, folks saying he was dead or gone back to his home planet or whatever the hell nutcase theory of the week. You didn't give him up either. Your boss must've chewed your ass good." Suddenly he paused, realizing. "Hey, that why you're here today? To warn me it's getting out? I know it can't be just bringin' an old man doughnuts."

"No, your privacy is still intact. Certainly as far as NPR is concerned. I admit that my producer and I discussed it. It was…" Now it was Christine who had a wry smile. "…well, it was spirited. But I finally persuaded him that both you and Justin had found… I don't know. A kind of accommoda-tion. Peace, even. And that we shouldn't ruin that for the sake of a story. Of course I was tempted by the thought of going public with Justin being Captain Dynamo, but…." She shrugged helplessly. "Honestly? I don't know why I backed off, exactly. I think I felt a little sorry for him. Remember what you told me about people the last time I was here?"

"What? That folks are just folks what really only want to live their lives? Even the supers?"

Christine nodded.

Voskovec chuckled. "I knew you must'a liked that one because you put it in the radio thing. Well, anyway, I figure I owe you something, kid, and not just for the doughnuts. Although bless your heart for bringin' em." He opened the bag and whistled. "Damn, a maple bar. You must want some-thing good." He pulled it out of the bag and admired it for a moment before taking a bite.

Christine was silent, letting him chew.

Voskovec finished the maple bar in moments and sighed with pleasure. Then he sat up a little and looked at Christine with his bright blue eyes. Christine had forgotten how powerful those eyes could be, clear and sharp and glittering with intelligence. They made him intimidating, even at his age and with him confined to a wheelchair.

Voskovec scowled, then grinned. "Okay then. So you don't want to give me up and you don't want to tell me some other reporter might do it. So what is it? What can Dr. Fixit do for you? Another radio story?"

"No. I'm not actually here for NPR today, this is for me." Christine hesitated. *Oh, hell, just tell him.* She took a deep breath and blurted, "I was hoping…. I thought maybe we could write a book."

"A book?" Ernie's eyebrows shot up. He looked genuinely surprised.

"I've been thinking about it ever since we did the original interview." Christine knew she was flushing again. She ignored it and plunged ahead, the words coming in a tumbling rush. "You're such a wonderful storyteller, and you operated as Dr. Fixit for… well, you said you started in 1956, right? And the Battle of Easter Sunday was 1968. Twelve years. And not just with Diamond Brain. You said you worked with the Midnight Midas, Devil-hound, Ocean Bandit, the Electric Ladyland Mob…. How many others?"

"Christ, I don't know. Practically all of them, I guess. Well, not Lizard King. That guy was a creep. Had a thing for underage… never mind. Nice girl like you don't need to hear about that. All I'm saying is, yeah, I was a crook but I had *standards.*" Voskovec shook his head. "You understand, I never was around for the costumes and fistfights and shit, though. Dr. Fixit was just what the villain guys called me; they were all so obsessed with giving everything a cool-sounding name. But it wasn't like I dressed up or wore a mask or nothing. I never made the papers. I just built stuff."

Christine had to laugh. "Ernie, you built *death rays.* And super vehicles and secret lairs and—God, I don't even know. But you were right there, in the thick of it. You must have stories."

Voskovec looked a little sheepish. "Well, yeah, I can't deny I saw some shit." His eyes drifted away from Christine, looking off into the distance. "You remember Ghostwalker?"

"Before my time. I'm twenty-two, Ernie."

Voskovec let out a brief, braying laugh. "Yeah, I guess so. You said super vehicles, it reminded me of the one hero job I ever did. Around 1962, I guess it woulda been. I know it was before the Beatles."

"A job for Ghostwalker?"

"Yeah." Now Voskovec was the one flushing. "I never told anybody this story, it woulda finished me in the business for sure, maybe even got me killed. But…" He let out a long sigh. " …I built the Ghostmobile."

Christine suppressed a giggle. *He said that like somebody admitting they worked in porn.* But she just said mildly, "Okay, *that's* got to be a story worth telling." She leaned forward and smiled. "I hope you understand, Ernie, it's not about me or my career or anything like that. I just think—there's a whole secret history here in St. Jacques City, one that people should know about. It's why I started researching the supers in the first place. And you know that history, Ernie, you lived it."

"Lived *through* it, more like." Voskovec made a sour face. "Even behind the scenes like I was, shit got scary sometimes. Ghostwalker—that was a hero job and it almost got me murdered. If you only knew…"

"But that's my point, Ernie." Christine looked at him and leaned forward. "I'd like to know. People *should* know."

Voskovec's brow furrowed. "Maybe," he said at last. "How are you thinking we'd do this?"

"We tape you again, to start. Not for the radio, just for me. Then I go home and write it up. You look at it and tell me any changes you think I should make. Rinse and repeat till we have a book." Christine added after a moment, "Strictly anonymous if that's how you want it. We can say it's *as-told-to*…well, whatever name you want to use."

"Don't you want your name on it either, kid?"

"I just want to do the book. I told you it's not about me. Of course I'd see to it you got paid."

Voskovec snorted, then smiled. "I know that, kid. You got a good heart. I trust you. It ain't that."

"Then what?"

He scowled and leaned back in the wheelchair. "Not sure, to be honest," he admitted. "Maybe… you keep saying people should know but maybe they don't *want* to know, see what I mean? Like the Ghostmobile job, it got pretty ugly toward the end."

"Tell me. You know by now I can take it." Christine smiled and pulled the tape recorder out of her purse. "In fact, let's just go ahead and roll tape and I'll write it up at home this week and then bring it back Saturday for you to say yes or no. It'll be our trial run. What do you say?"

"Hmm." Voskovec considered it. He hunkered down in his wheelchair, chin resting on one fist. His gaze drifted away from Christine into the remembering place, again. Then he sat up and nodded. "Sure. Let's try it. Most of these folks are gone now anyway. Even Ghostwalker's retired, finally. Anyway…" his teeth bared in the roguish grin again. "It really is the hell of a story. It happened like this…"

◎◎◎

Okay, I know you researched all this so you know the supers started with the Liberty Formula back in '42, during the war. You had the nuclear guys down in New Mexico and you had the bio-lab guys up here at Fort Wheeler, it's a museum now but it used to be an actual army base. The Fort

Wheeler guys hit on the serum that made Sergeant Smasher and Liberty Jane and the rest of the Liberty Brigade. I don't know what was in the books and clippings and so on you read, but the deal was they managed to create about, oh, somewhere between fifteen and twenty supers, I guess. Some of them went nuts; the formula did something to their brains, and one of them, called himself... I think it was Arclight, something like that. The electric guy. He decided what they was doing up at the lab there was against God or whatever and blew it all up in '44. Killed the scientist guys, burned the lab to the ground, then took himself out before the MPs even woke up enough to move in on him. And of course the Army covered it up, they didn't want Adolf's boys to know about the formula, that's why they put the Brigade in the masks and all in the first place. The idea was to sell the story that... okay, I see you nodding there. You know all this.

But the thing was, the Brigade, they stayed together after the war. Some of them did, anyway. It kind of got its own momentum going. It was Liberty Jane set the tone and the agenda, made it more about disaster rescue and citizen volunteer stuff like the Liberty Mission down there on Tenth—I think they're still on Tenth, I dunno, it's not like I get the newsletter.

And they fought crime. Street crime, mostly, they didn't have their act together enough to go after the serious mob guys. Though I think J. Edgar's boys might've tipped 'em on places they thought needed raiding but didn't have the evidence to get a warrant for it. Hoover had kind of a flexible relationship with due process sometimes, if you know what I'm sayin'.

So by the time I'm in the business, mid-fifties, Liberty Jane's retired, she's mostly running the foundation, the Brigade's a civilian thing. They had the headquarters up there on Lincoln Hill by the observatory.

And there were new members. The wartime folks are mostly gone by that point and now we're seeing this new breed, the science heroes. Remember them? Not supers, these were regular folks, but with tech that made 'em a match for any super. Ironmonger, Electric Eel, Jumping Jax, Firedancer. That crowd. They didn't get as much press as the wartime crew. Press didn't warm to 'em the way they did the Brigade. Though a lot of 'em were like, auditioning. The Brigade was still active. In fact they was supposed to be running point on the Bay of Pigs but Firedancer put the kibosh on that, she was half-Jamaican and she had a real bee in her bonnet about colonialist stuff, she liked Castro. She was one of the ones HUAC was looking at for a while there, but Hoover shut that down, he didn't want his pet supers dragged into no hearing.

Sergeant Smasher was still the leader; as late as 1960 he could still bench-press a trailer truck, and the first-generation supers didn't age as fast as regular folks. I'll tell you flat out, I can't prove it or nothing, but some of the guys used to talk about how the original wartime supers had faked dying and gone underground. Just to get away from the government trying to dissect them and get at the Liberty Formula, you know, recreate it somehow. Especially once a couple of bright Pentagon research guys realized it was possibly a way to immortality.

There were other rogue supers showing up too. Not Liberty Formula ones, either—radiation-based mutation gave us a couple. Cetacean, the fish guy, he was from the Bikini Islands where they did all that nuclear testing. Then there was the Indonesian kid, I forget his name but he could fly and he was a pyrokinetic too. He could point at a car or a warehouse or something and it'd just ignite. Not much control, though, and I don't think he lasted long. Warehouse explosion got him.

But sooner or later they all ended up here in St. Jacques City because the Brigade's here, see? So you'd get Firedancer or the Green Genie showing up in town beating on muggers or breaking up a bank robbery because they're tryin' to build a rep before auditioning for the Brigade. Some of them probably really was all civic-minded, but most of them were after the money and publicity, and everyone knew the Brigade was well-funded. Most folks thought it was still government.

Anyway. That's more or less where things were in '62 when Ghostwalker came on the scene. Nobody knew what the hell *his* story was. It started with guys getting dropped off at the police station—small-timers, muggers and whatnot—all tied up with a note saying what crime they did, signed with a little ghost cartoon saying BOO! Like this, gimme that pen, I can sketch it for you.

Nutty, right? But the *seriously* weird part is that these guys, they're already tied up and had the stuffing knocked out of 'em, bruised and bleeding, you'd think they'd be all pissed off and screaming about their rights. That's how it usually went when the mask-and-cape crowd pulled that shit. Sure, it's dramatic, made the papers, but the part that got left out is those gift-wrapped crooks all *walked* unless they were wanted for something else. Trussing 'em up and dropping 'em at the station an' then taking off like that, it just wasted everyone's time. Cops were never able to hold 'em. None of them union-suit characters ever would unmask and take it all the way to court. So vigilante busts like that, half the time cops never bothered booking 'em.

But the ones the ghost guy dropped off were different. They couldn't confess fast enough. They were terrified. *Please lock me up, it's the only way I'll be safe.* That's how it always went. They'd confess to stuff going back years, never mind what they did that night. And all they'd say about the guy what bagged 'em was that he wasn't human.

He was mostly working the docks and the bad neighborhoods down by Goldwater Beach—not far from the Liberty Mission, actually. People started to catch glimpses of him, there were a couple of fuzzy newspaper pics, things like that. Pretty soon folks started callin' him Ghostwalker and it stuck. Dressed all in gray, full face mask with a hood, and something that was either a cape or a robe or something, kinda swirling around him. That was all anybody knew. No weapons anyone ever saw but he could take out five or eight guys at a time just with his fists, in a fight it was like he was everywhere at once. Street crooks thought he was magic or something supernatural. News guys were floating all kinds of theories… One guy over at the PBS affiliate was absolutely convinced it was Devilhound who'd faked his own death and this was his comeback. I coulda told him it wasn't, because I was there when Devilhound bought it and *nobody* comes back from that… but that's another story.

Ghostwalker had everybody talking, that's my point. No possibility too weird for St. Jacques back then. You know, you already got a city full of superpowered people, nothing's off the table any more.

But Ghostwalker wasn't any of the things people were saying. I found out the hard way.

It started with Trav—you remember him, he was my broker, the guy what lined up jobs for me. We had a pretty intricate system worked out where people who needed their lair done or their laser guns recalibrated or whatever could get word to us, there was a drop box—not a P.O. box, an office down by Kincannon Square. Vacant, I never went there, it didn't even have furniture. It was just a place with a mail slot in the door and some bullshit name on the pebbled glass over it. But I rigged a secret entrance where Trav came up in an elevator from the sewer system underneath the building, and I had hidden cameras in the hall rigged to a motion sensor. The infrared see-in-the-dark kind, I mean. But mine were—well, never mind, I can see I lost you already. I get carried away talking about the technical part of things.

What I mean is, Trav and I had it worked out where no one knew how to get to me unless I let 'em. There was two things I paid him for. First was to keep his ear to the ground for guys needed my kind of skills. What you might call extra-legal engineering. Second was to get word to 'em that they

It was just a place with a mail slot in the door...

could send a note to the drop box explaining what they were after and I'd get in touch. Maybe. No guarantees. If it looked like something I could do—and it wasn't always, some of those guys wanted really crazy shit like a headquarters on an orbiting asteroid or something. But if it was something I could do, y'know, down here on Earth, I'd get back to 'em, or Trav would, we'd work out a price, and then I'd get into it. Once it was done I'd collect my fee and say so long and leave 'em to their big mad-science scheme. Mostly they'd crash and burn and end up doing hard time, some super'd swoop in and smash it all to hell. But by then I was long gone, off to the next one.

I see you giving me the eye. What?

Look, I *know* it was crooked. Of course it was. People got hurt from what I built, no question. But it was so much money… and we needed that money for Debbie, it wasn't like I was being greedy. She was already getting sick with the leukemia that finally got her. You want to talk about greedy; you shoulda' seen the hospital bills we were getting hit with. So don't be getting on your high horse about drawing the line till you're up against it like we were. Then you find out where your real line is. Mine was Debbie. Period the end.

I'm losing track of my story here. Oh yeah, the drop. Well, Trav and I used to meet at the tavern down the block from my apartment, little place called the Clover. Irish pub, like, that was their deal. Not really upscale but nice, lots of teak and brass and no band or jukebox or anything, you could just sit and have your beer in peace. They did a great roast beef sandwich too. We usually met there on Tuesdays.

Anyway, one Tuesday Trav comes in with a nervous expression and says, "I got a weird one. Lot of money but I don't know if you want it."

"I always want a lot of money. You know they got this bone marrow thing they want to try for Debbie. Let's have it."

Trav hands me the note. It says, **We are aware of your skills from various contacts of ours in the superhuman community. We need a man of your talent and discretion for a job that pays $10,000 on completion. But we must meet in person. Midnight, Thursday the 9th, Longmeadows Park, by the fountain.**

Two days. I shrugged and handed it back to him. "So?"

"Sounds hinky to me." Trav shook his head. "Like a setup."

"Like cops, you mean?" I snorted. "Cops even don't know we exist. Guys like you and me, we're just henching it. They want the headliners, not the support crew."

"Not cops. I was thinking Brigade maybe. You know Liberty Jane was on Jack Paar talking about urban cancer and whatever…"

I waved it off. "Naw. What this is, this is a guy who doesn't want to pay. 'On completion' is a dead giveaway. He thinks I'll build him his whatever and then he'll stiff me and what am I gonna do, sue him? Well, I dealt with his kind before and I still got paid. I know how to handle these guys, don't worry. You just gotta be ready for when they try and knife you." I grinned. "Not a problem. Ten grand's too big not to at least take a look. I'll go. But…" I winked at him. "I'll be ready. Rest your mind. Hard part's going to be explaining being out so late to Debbie, that's all. But I managed that before too."

Trav nodded, still looking uneasy.

If I'd known what was coming, I'd'a been uneasy too. But at that point it was only a job, one more super-widget for one more super-weirdo. Just another day at the office for me.

◎◎◎

I tried never to out-n-out lie to Debbie. I just left stuff out so she wouldn't worry. She was a good Methodist girl and she wouldn't a'liked me working for crooks, even though I wasn't committing no crimes. Well, not technically, anyway. I mean, it's not illegal to build stuff. Though I gotta admit we kinda' skirted the edges when it came to zoning and OSHA laws and such, and I think it's probably some kind of crime if you're knowingly doing business with somebody on the Ten Most Wanted list.

But mostly, everything *I* did as Doc Fixit, I made sure I was in the clear. I had incorporated as a small business, I made sure I got paid by cashier's check so's I'd have a paper trail for the IRS—yeah, I paid taxes. I mean, come on. I'd risk my neck working for Steel Spectre, sure, but only a damn fool plays footsie with the tax man. And doing it that way, it worked same as cash, clients wouldn't have anything leading to them, so they didn't get nervous on their end. I tried to think of everything. I was always—*always*—damn careful. Just because my customers were mental cases in weird suits don't mean they weren't *dangerous*.

But there was no point in burdening my Debbie with all of that. "Got to meet a guy and look at some work he wants done," I told her. "I'm afraid I'm gonna be late. Might end up being a month or two of night work if I take it."

"Oh, Ernie." She gave me a hug. "You work too hard."

"We need the money, you know we do." I pulled her close and kissed her, and let my chin rest on the top of her head for a moment. Then I pulled back and looked at her. "Don't you worry about me. How you feeling? Them pills helping?"

"Some. I don't like them, though, they make me all draggy."

"I don't like you hurting." I scowled. "You take one if you need to. There ain't no points for being all heroic. This ain't a movie and you ain't John Wayne."

"I know." She sighed and for a moment she looked so bleak and sad I got a lump in my throat like I might start crying.

Instead I swallowed it back and said, "Anyway, I gotta get out to meet this guy. Don't wait up."

"Eat something. Something healthy," she added, and this smile wasn't bleak. "Not those greasy burgers from the drive-in."

"All right. For you I'll get a salad at the deli." I kissed her and went.

Okay, that was a little lie I told, yeah, but it made Debbie happy so screw it. Truth is, I didn't go to the deli. Eating made me sleepy and for a first meet I needed to be sharp.

Instead I drove to the outskirts of Longmeadows and suited up. I didn't have a costume, but I had what I called my work clothes. Basic mechanic's coverall. Black electrician's gloves, thin cloth with rubber-coated fingers. Tool belt with a couple of useful electronic gizmos tucked away in the pouches along with my screwdriver and hammer and wrenches. And my goggles I'd rigged special, that also served to hide my face some. Nothing that said *costumed crook* to any cop that happened by and I had a story for any that did. But in my work duds I was as dangerous as any supervillain, if I needed to be.

I parked a ways away from the fountain, left my wallet and ID locked in the car, and walked the rest of the way. Slow approach, checking it out. I tapped the side of my goggles, activating the night vision.

The guy waiting by the fountain was standing ramrod straight, briefcase in hand, dressed in a business suit and wearing a gray fedora hat. He would have looked like a banker or something except for two things; the briefcase was chained to his wrist and he was wearing a black domino mask.

He heard me coming up on him and turned to face me with a thin smile showing no teeth. "Ah. Doctor Fixit? I see you are dressed for work." Faint British accent. Definitely a limey but one who'd been living here in the States for a while.

"I'm a working guy."

"Indeed." The smile got a little wider, a little thinner, but still no teeth. "I have ten thousand dollars in bearer bonds in this briefcase. If we come to terms I unlock the cuff chaining it to my wrist and it's all yours. Shall we discuss the job?"

"First let's discuss your pal over there." I nodded towards the other side of the fountain. "That's a good screen but I'm not some mugger. I done light-bending work myself, I know an invisibility shimmer when I see it." I admit I was bluffing a little. It was the night-vision infrared in my goggles what put me on to him; no matter how good your holograms are, they can't hide your heat signature. But it was better to keep 'em guessing. "I don't have time for games. He's hanging back so I'm guessing he's the boss. Let's talk face to face if we're going to talk business. Like I said, I'm a working guy and it's past my bedtime." I looked past the limey and addressed the shimmer. "I'm here like you asked. Let's get to it."

A new voice came, layered on top of itself with lots of reverb. "Clearly, your reputation is deserved."

It sounded spooky, yeah, but I knew what a throat mic was. This guy was strictly science-based, no superpowers that I could see. This was all stage-magic stuff.

Proving my point, there was a swirl of smoke and then there he was. I was getting probably the first good look at him anyone ever had, thanks to my goggles. Hooded, with a full face mask, and white orbs where his eyes should be. Some kinda opaque lenses. What people said was a cape or a robe was really a long gray silk coat, same cut as a leather duster, with sleeves that got wide at the end. He was wearing gloves, a little darker gray than the coat and the mask.

I blinked. "You're the boo boy from the papers. Ghostwalker, right?"

He nodded and pointed at me. "And you are the famous Doc Fixit."

I started to get a little nervous. "Yeah. I gotta say, I don't usually get calls from your side of the street."

"Is that going to be a problem?" Whatever enhancements he'd used with the mic, it really was a damn spooky voice. That and the smoke made it a convincing act.

Just tech, I reminded myself. *Don't let him rattle you.* "No problem here," I tried to keep the quaver out of my voice. "So what's the job? Are you here to do business or not?"

"We'll do business. But not here." Ghostwalker waved his hand again and everything around me started to shimmer. Not optics this time. Son of a bitch was using gas. *Some kind of mist pump on his back, hose runs down the sleeve and spray nozzles built into the gloves,* I thought, blearily. Even passing out, I was still thinking like an engineer.

Black crept in around the edges of my vision and I had the distant sensation I was falling forward, but I was out before I hit the ground.

⊚⊚⊚

I came to in a white room with no windows. I could hear the faint whooshing sound of a ventilation system but with no vents I could see. Normally when somebody gasses you, you wake up with the mother of all hangovers. But I felt okay. Just a little weak and shaky. Whatever he was using, it was the good stuff. High-end, KGB level. I knew our military didn't have chemicals that sophisticated but the Russians did. I hoped to Christ this wasn't some international thing. I didn't mind helping out the bank robbers and so on but political stuff was guaranteed trouble.

"Doctor?" The limey's voice.

I sat up and rubbed my eyes. I was still in my work outfit, but they'd taken the goggles and the tool belt. I was on a cot set against one wall of the white room. Featureless except for a door set flush in the wall at the far end.

I saw the limey leaning on a workbench against the wall on the opposite side from me. He'd shucked the jacket and fedora, but still was in the shirt and tie. And of course the domino mask.

"Where's my stuff?" I asked him.

"Right here." He moved aside and I could see my belt and goggles on the workbench behind him. "Everything is intact. We were concerned about some kind of homing tracker, because we need this location to remain secret."

"You think I can't keep secrets? For Chrissake, d'you think I'd have lasted as long as I have without keeping my trap shut? I know stuff about folks you wouldn't..."

He held up a hand. "I believe you. Truly." He paused for a moment and looked almost embarrassed. Then he went on, more firmly, "But we intend to last as well, however, and you must understand that means taking precautions. We had to be sure you weren't carrying anything that broadcast a signal. If we can put this initial awkwardness behind us, I assure you, we still want to hire you."

I jabbed a finger at him. "I got conditions. You better hear me out before we go any further."

He nodded and gestured for me to go ahead.

"Okay." I drew in a long breath and let it out slow. "First, you never gas me again. Blindfold, bag over the head, whatever, I ain't interested in where you hide your secret headquarters. But no gas."

"Of course…"

"I mean fear gas too."

He blinked and I could see the startled expression even behind his mask.

I snorted and went on, "For God's sake. Your guy must be spoiled dealing with muggers and small-timers. Get it through your head, I been *around*, all right? I know the tricks. I could feel whatever he uses working on me before he let loose the sleepy stuff. Nozzles in the gloves, right? Some kind of…. I dunno, I'm not a chemical engineer. But it works on the fight-or-flight response, got to be something like that. Some kinda nerve agent."

The limey was looking at me with new respect. "Indeed. You are very astute."

"I was already thinking it must be something like that from the news stories." I waved it away. "It's not new. Steel Spectre used to use a gimmick like that, but his was mechanical. Subsonics. We could never lick the power curve on it, though, so he only was able… never mind. That's not the point. The point is, if we are going to do business, you treat me with some goddamn *respect*. I'm not some ignorant stickup man. I'm a professional. Save the spook act for the rubes."

The door at the far end of the room opened and Ghostwalker strode in. Still all suited up, but he didn't bother with the smoke effects this time. "Very well, Doctor," he said. No reverb in it. *He must have been listening in,* I thought, and it was confirmed when he added, "Those conditions are acceptable."

"I ain't done." I glared at him.

"Oh?" Ghostwalker crossed his arms and nodded at me to continue. He sounded amused. Beside him, the masked limey was looking a little nervous.

I ignored it. This was a job and I was a pro. "You want to keep your secrets. I understand that. I'm going to need some things, though. Whatever you want done, if you called me, it means there's going to be some serious engineering involved, right? Metalworking, electronics, machining parts probably, who knows what-all. You got ways to get that stuff here? We working on-site? Because if I have to figure out all that too, it's going to mean more money. Not just for me, I mean basic capital expenditure." I shrugged. "On the other hand, you just want a consult, I'm happy to take a look, but I'm thinking ten grand means hands-on. So ten grand's probably just the beginning. It ain't just me that's gonna cost you."

Ghostwalker nodded. "A reasonable assessment." He turned to the limey. "I think he'll do. See to the details." He spun around without waiting for an answer and swept out of the room.

The door closed with a soft click and I chuckled. "Well. He's a little full of himself, ain't he? But I guess all these costume guys are." I faced the limey. "Where do you fit in to all this, anyway? You been working for him all along?"

"I suppose you could say I once had your job." He smiled a little ruefully at me. "I'm something of an engineer myself, but…." He held out a hand and I could see it trembling. "My health doesn't permit me to do the fine detail work the way I used to."

I winced. "Palsy?"

"Technically it's called Parkinson's Disease. There is no cure." He sighed. "It's not too bad. Eventually I will be in a wheelchair, I imagine, but for now, I can manage… for the most part. My intellect is not hampered. I can't use my hands the way I used to, that's all. So much of the work I do here involves concealment and miniaturization. I can't do the subtle things any more." Again with the rueful smile. "So I persuaded the master to let me hire some help. I realize our approach was a bit unconventional, and perhaps discourteous, but…."

"It's the business we're in. I get it." I kinda liked him, I decided. His boss mighta been a jerk but this Brit seemed like a decent guy. "Fair enough. Let's talk about the job. But if we're going to be working together, I'd just as soon use real names. You can call me Ernie."

That was the first time I got a genuine smile out of him, one with teeth. He reached up and took off his mask. "All right. I'm Alastair."

"Nice to meetcha." We shook hands. "So what's the job?"

"Ah, that will involve some explaining. If you can follow me…"

I stood up. "First you gotta let me call my wife. She's gonna wonder why I ain't home yet. I don't care if you listen in but no trace, okay?"

"No trace. My word." Alastair flashed me another smile. "We won't trouble the master with it. After all, we are both professionals."

With that, I knew he was my kinda guy, in spite of the plummy accent. When you're henching, you get a feel for what stuff you tell the boss and what stuff you don't bother him about. I guess it worked that way on the hero side of things too.

He gestured at the workbench for me to reclaim my tool belt and goggles. I put 'em back on and checked the pouches on the belt. Everything there. I pushed the goggles back up on my head and nodded at Alastair. "Okay. Phone?"

He led me out through the door to a white hallway, lit with fluorescents. Like in an office building, but a little too bright. He pointed at a small alcove and I saw a phone sitting there. White too, of course. "Dial 9 to get an outside line."

I nodded and picked up the handset. "How long has it been, anyway? What time is it now?"

Alaistair consulted a pocket watch. The guy was an old-fashioned Brit to his toes. "A little after five AM."

"Okay." I hated waking her up but I knew if Debbie woke up on her own with me not there, she'd be in a panic. I moved to where my back was to Alastair and dialed. Standing that way he couldn't see me palm a silver disc from my front belt pouch and slide it under the phone. When I felt the magnet click into place I felt better. I liked the guy but that didn't mean I trusted him, not yet. And I sure didn't trust his boss. Insurance never hurts.

I heard the burr of the phone ringing on Debbie's end. She picked up right away. Damn it, she must have been waiting up. "Ernie, is that you? Are you all right?"

"I'm fine, honey, just checking in. This is taking longer than I thought it would, that's all."

"I'm glad to hear from you. I was worried,"

"I know. I'm sorry. Time got away from me." I glanced at Alastair. He had the grace to look embarrassed. "Anyway, it all looks fine. I think the job's going to work out. Shouldn't be too much longer. You should go back to bed."

"I can't sleep till you get here."

"At least try. For me."

"All right." She added, "You worry about me all the time, I'm allowed to worry about you too."

"Nothing to worry about. It's just another job. You go to bed now. I love you."

"I love you too. Be safe."

I hung up and turned to face Alastair. "Okay?"

He nodded, his expression looking a little wistful. "It's for her, isn't it? The work you do, the risks you take. She must be something special."

"She is." I was curt. I didn't want to talk about Debbie. So I diverted. "What about your guy? How'd you get mixed up with him?"

Alastair could divert too. He sighed. "Oh we all make our devil's bargain, I suppose. Anyway, come along, let's take a look at the work you're here for." He led us to the end of the hall through another door, this one heavier-duty than the others. Then he turned and gestured for me to precede him. I shrugged and went on through.

It was bigger than a garage but smaller than a hangar, and it looked like it could function as either. Concrete floor and corrugated metal siding on all sides, with two big doors at one end. Still no windows, just lots of racks and machinery and tools. In the center was something that looked like a car, or at least the skeleton of a car, with an engine hanging from a crane over the front and various pieces of the chassis sort of scattered around it, all the same cloud-gray as Ghostwalker's outfit. Off to one side I could see another workbench piled high with electronics and wiring.

Suddenly I got it. "Oh man," I breathed, and my face lit up with this big grin like a kid in a candy store.

"What?" Alastair had looked startled at first, then wryly amused. "Is something funny?"

"Your boss," I chuckled. "He's just a big kid underneath all the spook-show act. He wants a tricked-out rod. Right? All this cloak-and-dagger for a cool car?"

Alastair harrumphed. "I have designed it to be the ultimate stealth urban operational vehicle, infinitely maneuverable with multiple defense and offense capabilities." One corner of his mouth pulled up in another thin-lipped smile. "But yes, with your help, Doctor—Ernie—I expect the Ghost-mobile shall be a *very* cool car."

◎◎◎

It didn't take long to work out a routine. We met weeknights around ten, Longmeadows Park, same as the first time. Alastair'd pick me up in a limo, and I'd get in the back. He'd roll up the privacy screen and pull out. Windows were blacked out so no need for sleep gas, though I had my nose filters in all the time anyway. Fool me once and all that. But there was never any trouble or tricks.

I have to admit this was my favorite kinda job to work on. I always was a car guy, and this kind of hands-on labor was hugely relaxing for me: something like this took my mind off Debbie being so sick, I could just get lost in the job. Believe it or not, in all my years as Doc Fixit, this was the first time I'd ever actually got to work on a real car. Subs, hovercraft, even tanks, sure. But never just a cool car. I guess underneath it all I was a big kid too.

It was great to get in there with my tools and build this thing. Alastair's blueprints were very thorough; he'd already solved most of the practical problems at the design stage. The guy was just brilliant, that's all there was to it. Damn shame about the palsy, but even with that he coulda wrote his own ticket at any of the big outfits. Boeing, Lockheed, hell, he coulda retired at forty just on the patents for things he'd figured out for this supercar.

But then, in our line of work, patents weren't really a factor. I suppose you could say the same thing about me. I guess I coulda got out of the business if I really tried. I didn't have a college degree and my proudest accomplishments as an engineer were for stuff I couldn't a'never put on a legit employment application. But I might have gone legit if I'd put my mind to it. The thing is, me and Debbie were always just kinda living from one medical panic to the next, and I already had a solution that was working. Why rock the boat?

Alastair's designs were seriously next-level stuff, though. I couldn't see why he'd play second fiddle to a nut in a ghost outfit. The few times I'd asked him about it, he brushed me off the same way I'd done him with talking about Debbie. Well, fair enough. People in the business always had reasons. I had mine, he had his. Whatever. I let it go.

I wasn't really worrying, not at first. This gets lost in all the news reports about the supers and the villains, but the work I was doing, well… it was *fun*. This Ghostwalker job especially. I mean, the job was to basically build the world's coolest car, right? How can you not love that? Also, I hardly ever got to work with someone that was on my level, but Alastair was…. I gotta be honest here. He was better than me. I was learning a lot. The things he had doped out about miniaturization…

Look. You gotta understand, in the late fifties, early sixties, it was always a war between power and portability. It doesn't matter if you got a raygun that can carve up a bank vault if the generator running it is so huge you can't even get it loaded into a pickup. The power demands go sky-high for that kind of thing and all these villain guys were after something handheld. I'd tried all kinds of things over the years, solar chargers, mirror-stacked laser remotes, any kind of crackpot notion that could give you a lot of juice that didn't have to draw off the city grid, something you could pick up and take with you.

The Ghostmobile was kinda that problem, but doubled down, because we had to run a car engine along with all the weapons systems. And we had to do it without weighing it down so heavy that it'd never go faster'n twenty miles an hour. I don't know if I'd have ever figured it out on my own, but Alastair's solution was elegant. Once we got to work on it I realized it wasn't a car engine at all. "This is like a jet," I said. "A plane, but with wheels instead of wings?"

"After a fashion." Alastair looked pleased. "Except we don't burn fuel. Batteries are charged from the miniature atomic pile and the intakes up front bring in the air to spin the turbines. We have a brief pause for the initial power-up but then it should run for days without any need to recharge." His brow furrowed. "Honestly the difficulty is reining it in. It's vastly overpowered for regular street driving, and masking the hoverjet noise has been deeply frustrating."

"We can't get the turbines any quieter." I considered it. "You already got the chassis configured almost like a wing, the faster it goes the more lift the car gets, so there's that much less power demand on the engine. Get it up on plane like a speedboat, almost. That helps a little. Highway's no problem, it's city driving you have to worry about. Maybe add a set of baffles to the exhaust, or even some kind of sonic array... I don't know the word for it. White sound, I think they called it when I was figuring out Steel Spectre's death maze. He had kind of a ghost schtick too, so he was all about keeping his gizmos quiet. There's a trick with sonics where you find frequencies what cancel each other out, like." I scowled. "I wish I'd wrote that stuff down back then, but you know how these guys get about paper trails. Still..."

A new voice broke in. "Hey, Al, who's the new guy?"

The voice was coming from what I thought at first was some kind of Ghostwalker stunt double, a masked-and-costumed kid that sounded no older than nineteen or twenty. But on second look there were differences between his look and Ghostwalker's. His outfit was a little tighter, almost like something a gymnast would wear, and the hood didn't cover his whole head, the top was cut off so you could see tousled brown hair. The eyes were the same kind of white opaque lenses, but the swirly cape thing really was a cape, not a jacket, with the ends attached at the wrists. He looked more like a circus aerialist than anything. But his outfit was definitely patterned after Ghostwalker.

"I'm Ernie," I said. "And you are?"

"Code names only," Alastair put in before the kid could answer. He turned to me and smiled apologetically. "You understand, of course. This young man is my ward and I'm charged with his safety."

I could hear the kid snort and I imagine his eyes were rolling behind

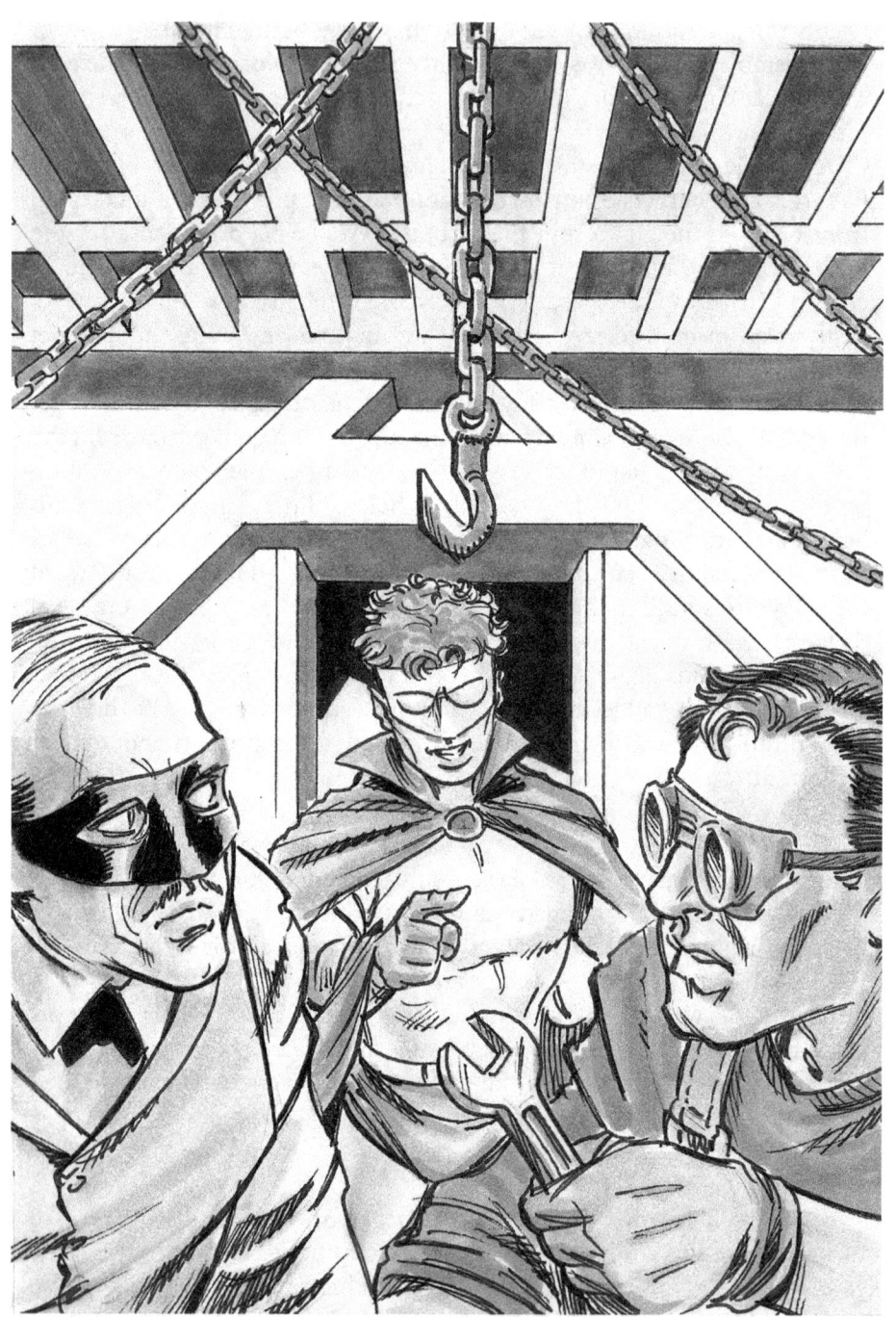

"Hey, Al, who's the new guy?"

the mask. "You worry too much, Al. All right. Code names it is. That was actually why I came down, tell the truth."

Down. I filed that away in the little mental dossier I was building on this outfit. I'd suspected this garage-workshop-whatever space was underground. Nice to have it confirmed.

Alastair crossed his arms and smiled wryly at the kid. "We're back to this?"

"I'm not calling myself Ghost Boy."

"We have to call you something,"

"How about Kid Ghost?" I asked. "Like a boxer."

"Hmmm." Alastair looked at me, interested. "That is better, I must say."

But the caped kid just made a noise of frustration. "That's not the point. I don't want anything about Boy or Kid in the name *at all*. I'm not a kid any more, Al."

"Until you're twenty-one you are, and under my care." Alaistair's voice had the tiniest little edge in it. "You insist on accompanying the master on his patrols, despite my objections. There's little I can do about it, seeing as how he has approved. But…"

I could tell Alastair was getting a little lost in the weeds, and the moment was getting awkward. I decided to rescue them both from the family quarrel it was shaping up to become. "Look here," I said to the kid. "You're making too much of it. The name don't matter that much as long as folks remember you. Call yourself Spookster or Revenant or Gravedigger or whatever. You don't want to get mixed up with anybody else is all. So I'd leave out anything with 'ghost' in it, save that one for your partner. Same with 'spectre,' because a' Steel Spectre. But there's lotsa' other ghostly names out there. Just pick one."

"Gravedigger sounds kinda cool," the kid admitted.

"And it's got assonance," Alaistair added.

"What?" The kid sounded confused.

"Rhythm," I told him. "Ghostwalker and Gravedigger. Both start with G, both end with R, three syllables each. You get words what pair up like that but don't rhyme, it's called assonance."

"Hey, you're right. That's pretty smart." There was new respect in the kid's voice. Then it became rueful. "Not paired up tonight, though. Big guy benched me."

"Oh?" I said, innocently. Small talk, but I was always looking to add to the dossier. Like I said, in my business, liking folks has nothing to do with trusting 'em.

Alastair shot him a warning look but it sailed right by the kid. "Yeah, he said he was going after Serpentina. Too dangerous for me."

"That's enough, young man." Alastair's voice had an edge in it. "Run along upstairs and get out of that uniform, since you're not going out." His voice softened a little. "I'll be along in a bit. We can talk about design improvements to reflect your new name."

"Okay, Al. Sounds good." The kid bounded out. He moved like a human spring, energy just came off him in waves.

"Thank you for that," Alastair said to me after the kid was gone. "The young master is somewhat irrepressible."

"Ain't nothing," I said, but I was only half-listening. My mind was in a whirl.

Tina? What the hell did this spookshow outfit want with Tina?

⊚⊚⊚

I knew Serpentina, see. Got acquainted with her back in the Devilhound days. She'd been part of the Reptile Squad, Lizard King's outfit. But she saw what a creep he turned out to be and jumped ship over to Devilhound's gang while I was doing his lair, and we got to be friends. Mostly because I was the only guy there that wasn't putting the make on her. She was a knockout—the best kind of pretty, the kind where she doesn't hardly even know it. No vanity to her.

Her schtick was climbing—not a super, just a world-class gymnast, 'cept the whole city was her parallel bars, like. You shoulda' seen her slither up a fire escape and whip across an alley five stories up, going from a flagpole to a window ledge to a chimney like it was nothing. She was Olympic material, easy. I helped her out a bit back in the day; fixed her up with a little collapsible grapnel line she could wear on her belt, and gloves with vacuum suction for going up glass-front skyscrapers, which were starting to be a thing here starting around '58. Nice kid. But she'd quit Devilhound about the same time I did, and I heard she went straight. Even in her heyday she wasn't any kind of real danger to folks, her thing was burglary. Jewels were her specialty but she was good with industrial espionage too.

I couldn't figure out why Ghostwalker was chasing her but I thought it wouldn't hurt to give her a heads-up. Tina wasn't really equipped to take on a heavy hitter like him, especially with his fear gas gimmick.

I thought finding her might be a problem but all it took was a phone call to Trav. He kept tabs on folks; that was one of the things I paid him for.

Networking, I guess you kids call it now. Course it helped I knew her real name. All most hoods knew was "Serpentina" but I knew she was really just Tina Jankewicz from the South side.

Debbie usually napped in the afternoon after she took her pills, so I told her I was going to run a couple of errands. I did need to pick up some thin high-tension cable, just a little spool of the stuff. Alastair and I were playing with an idea for a sort of electric-net gun we could mount on the front of the Ghostmobile. Alastair was adamant we stick with non-lethal hardware, and I remembered the tanglewire trap I'd figured out for the Midnight Midas. Just had to figure out how to mount the—well, never mind all that. But it gave me an excuse to be out and around and it wasn't any trouble to stop by Tina's place after.

It turned out to be a fourth-floor walkup not too far from the riverfront, only about ten blocks or so from Longmeadows as it turned out. Kinda run-down, but clean. Climbing the stairs I could hear kids laughing and old guys arguing and all sorts of stuff; walls musta' been paper-thin. The smell of boiled cabbage permeated the hallway. Reminded me of Debbie's and my first place back in '49, before I fell into the Doc Fixit thing and we was able to buy a house.

When Tina opened the door her eyes went wide and her face split in a delighted grin. She wrapped me in a big hug. "Ernie! Oh my God it's been years. Come in, come in. How are you? How's your wife?"

We made small talk for a couple of minutes. There's always the uncomfortable part where I had to explain about Debbie being sick. Not going into all kinds of detail or anything, but you gotta tell people something. So I gave her the short version that made it sound better than it was, then added, "Truth is, kid, I ain't here just to catch up. I want you to tell me the truth, now. You back in the business?"

Tina looked away for a second. Now it was her that was uncomfortable. Finally she said, "Sort of. I mean, it's going to just be a one-off, but… God, Ernie, I'm so embarrassed. I've made such a mess of things. I don't even know where to start."

"You know this Ghostwalker guy is gunning for you."

That shocked her, but not the way I thought. "How did you know about him? That was just a few nights… oh, hell." Then she busted out crying.

I felt like an idiot. I don't know what I was thinking would happen but this wasn't it. I just held her and said stupid things like *Hey*, and *It's gonna be all right*, until the storm passed.

Finally she pushed me away and went to sit on an old overstuffed couch.

"Boy, if the Reptiles could see me now." She let out a bitter laugh.

"What is it, honey?" I asked her. "What's up with Ghostwalker? He trying to send you up? Some kind of publicity bust? You been out of the game for a while, what's the point?"

Tina shook her head. "He's blackmailing me."

"What? How? What's he got on you?"

Then the bedroom door opened and a voice said, "Mommy? I heard voices." A little curly-headed blonde girl in a pink jumper emerged from the bedroom.

"Hi sweetie, I hope you had a nice nap." Tina smiled wanly and added, "This is Sarah, Ernie. My daughter."

So then I knew exactly what Ghostwalker had on her. One phone call to the feds and Sarah loses her mommy. With that to hold over Tina's head, he owned her.

⊙⊙⊙

I ended up bringing Tina and her daughter back home with me for dinner. "The spook won't find you at our place, and Debbie'd love to see you. It'll be a break for you and it buys me some time to figure out how to help you. Just remember," I added, "No work talk, at dinner, y'know what I mean? Far as Debbie's concerned I'm in construction, engineering. Contract work."

That got another bitter laugh out of Tina. "Well, it's true, isn't it?"

"Exactly."

Dinner turned out to be a good call for everybody. Debbie was more herself than she'd been for months, with Tina and especially little Sarah to fuss over. My wife loved kids, it was a damn crime she wasn't able to have any.

We had a spare room with a sofa, and other odds and ends. Kind of a craft room; it was mostly where Debbie did her sewing. My wife had it all figured out. She told Tina, "We can put you on the couch and the little one can make do on the floor. Like camping, but inside, right sweetie?" This last was to Sarah.

"Yay, camping!" Sarah was all over that. Debbie laughed, her first real laugh in a year, I think. And even Tina giggled.

After dinner I gave Debbie the high sign that she should take Sarah out of the room so Tina and I could talk. So she and Sarah went back to the spare room to liven up the camping festivities with more refinements.

"Blanket fort, I think," Debbie said.

"What's a blanket fort?" Sarah wanted to know.

"The best thing ever," Debbie assured her, and they disappeared back into the craft room.

I raised an eyebrow at Tina. "You look like you could stand to hide out in a blanket fort yourself, kid."

"I miss life being simple. Even in the old days, climbing buildings and running from cops and all, it was still just me. A kid comes into your life and everything changes." She sighed. "I wouldn't trade Sarah for the world, but it's not just me, alone, any more, you know? I have to think through everything."

"Her dad's not in the picture at all, then."

"Not since '59." Tina's smile was wan. "Ricky was smart and handsome and fun, but not really daddy material. Met him when we were both Reptile Guard. He stayed when I left and it all just kind of fell apart. There was no way we were going to get married. He did send us money, he might have come around to going domestic with us, but he got killed in that big showdown at the Mint." She shrugged. "I don't hold a grudge. It's who he was. It's been me and Sarah against the world all along. I'm used to it."

"Does Sarah know?"

"Just that he's gone. I told her he died on the job. Accident. It's true enough. The rest can wait till she's older." She sighed and smiled at me. "I guess that's the kind of smoothed-over truth you tell Debbie, huh?"

"Kind of." This was a road I didn't want to go down. "So how'd you get back into the life?"

"I didn't." Tina's eyes flashed with anger. "It's that Ghost bastard, he's pushing me back in."

"What does he want?"

"He wants me to knock off Reichenbach Motors. Simple really, office safe with plans, but it's in a penthouse. Locked off from the main building, private elevator. It's an industrial job. You know, they're the ones that..."

"That make the fancy sports cars," I finished.

She nodded.

I had that feeling you get when you're looking at a big engineering problem, something with a lot of moving parts but you can't get it solved because there's a couple things you can't see. I turned the pieces around in my head, trying to figure how they fit. Burglary. Supers. A hero that maybe wasn't. Using a villain proxy. And this supercar me and Alistair were building. It all fit together, somehow, I knew it did, but I couldn't see it. Not quite.

"You kids should stay here for a couple days," I told her. "Buy you some time away from Big Bad Boo. Let me see if I can get a handle on this for you."

I thought she was gonna fight me on it, but she agreed with relief. Ghost-walker really had her wound up tight. I was pretty sure there was stuff she hadn't told me but I wasn't gonna lean on her when she was so obviously terrified. Instead, I got up to go get my work duds on. It was getting time to get myself over to Longmeadows to meet Alastair and the limo.

Debbie came out to join us and as she came to me, Tina went back to the craft room to see how Sarah was doing. Debbie smiled at her over her shoulder and then put her arms around my waist and turned to me. "That's a sweet little girl. Both of them are."

"Tina was always a good kid. Just had some bad luck."

Debbie looked up at me with steel in her eyes. I knew that look. She'd made up her mind. "We need to help them, Ernie."

That was my girl. Once she'd decided you were family, it was ride or die all the way. "I'm going to do what I can," I told her.

"It's a man, isn't it? Poor little girl, raising a daughter all alone, she's easy prey. No, I don't need to know the details. She needs a break from worrying about it. And you need to run along to work, mister." She gave my butt an affectionate pat. "You can tell me everything later."

"Will do." I grinned at her and went back to the bedroom to get my coveralls. *Maybe I really should tell her everything,* I thought for the millionth time. *One of these days I will.*

◎◎◎

In spite of everything I was excited to get back to Alastair and the garage that night because we were about ready for the first test run. The car was built and we'd figured on taking it out to the hills east of town and seeing what it could really do.

I should have known better.

I could tell something was off from when Alastair picked me up. I said something about finally the big night being here and all he did was grunt. British gentlemen don't grunt; Alastair *never* grunted. So I knew something was up. But, you know, in the trade, we don't ask questions. I figured it was another family squabble over the kid and forgot about it.

I almost had it right. The awkward squabble between the spook and Alastair wasn't about Junior. Apparently it had been about me.

When we arrived and I got out of the blacked out limo, the garage was mostly dark except for a small circle of light next to the completed Ghost-mobile. In the center of the circle stood Ghostwalker, in his full regalia.

I set down my reel of wire and sighed. *These costume freaks are all such drama queens. Well, whatever it is, let's not put it off.* "What's up, boss man?" I asked him.

He nodded at Alastair. "Give us the room for a moment." Alaistair inclined his head and disappeared out the side door.

Ghostwalker turned to me. "Alastair tells me the work is completed. He has nothing but high praise for you. I appreciate that. You have done well. If anything, your reputation is understated."

"Well, thanks." I cocked an eyebrow at him. "So shall we settle up? Ten grand was the agreement."

Ghostwalker gave me a slow nod. "There has been some discussion about that. Alastair has persuaded me that I owe you something for your labor. Here is one thousand in cash." He held out an envelope.

I ignored it and glared at him. "And the rest?"

He was smirking behind that full face mask, I could *feel* it. "The rest is, shall we say, barter. Favors."

"Favors?" I could feel the bristling edge in my voice and didn't care. I *knew* the sonofabitch would try and weasel.

"First, we keep it between us that you helped a crimefighter. That would be deadly in your profession. Especially once I let it be known that Doctor Fixit is Ernie Voskovec. Married to Debra. Lives in the suburbs in a tan split-level two-bedroom." A dry little chuckle. "I think keeping that information to myself is more than worth the difference in payment, don't you? Did you really think I wouldn't find out who you really are? I knew before I ever hired you. I make it my business to know everything about the people who work for me, Voskovec. *Everything.*"

I said two words. The first one I wouldn't repeat in front of a lady. The second was *you.* I added, "All right, you got all the cards. But don't kid yourself. You're no hero. Scrape the paint off, you're just like every other rich bastard I ever met. A pushy no-talent making it on the backs of people way better than you, just because you got money and they don't. Your boy Al is worth ten of you."

That got to him. The voice hardened. "Watch yourself, Voskovec. You might talk yourself out of even this courtesy payment. Remember your wife."

My wife was the only reason I didn't whip out one of a dozen disguised

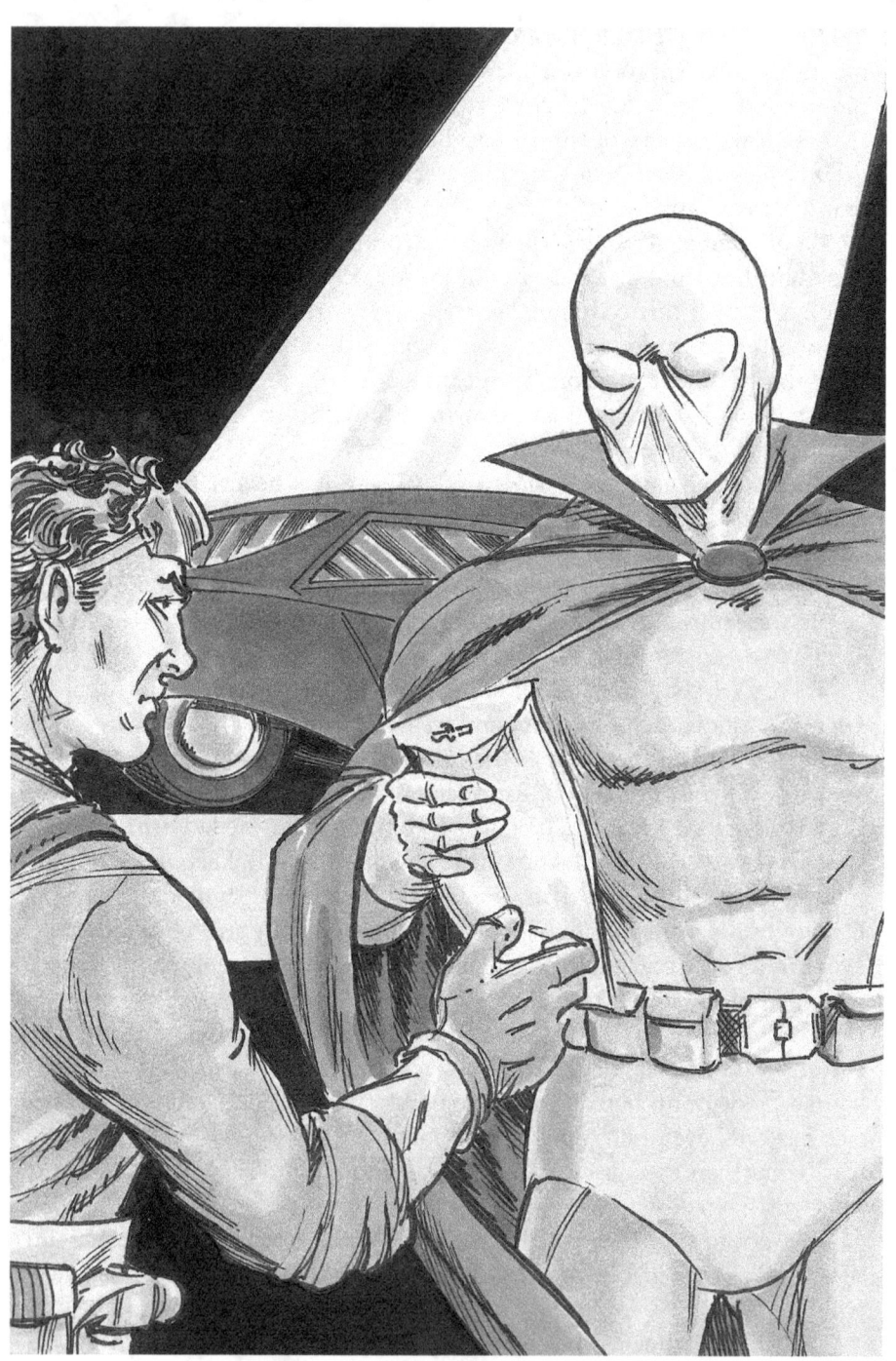

*He was smirking behind that full face mask, I could **feel** it.*

weapons in my tool belt and let him have it. This bastard would get what was coming to him, but on *my* terms, after I'd made sure there wouldn't be nothing coming back on Debbie. Remember, I'd been at this a while, so it wasn't exactly a surprise the smug sonofabitch would try to welch on me. Hell, I'd told Trav as much when he came to me about the approach. But with Debbie at risk, I had to play it careful.

Still, I couldn't keep the anger out of my voice. "All right. You win. Is that what you want to hear? You got me by the balls. We both know it. Just quit gloating and let me out of here."

Some signal must have passed, because Alastair was suddenly back again. Neither one of us said anything. He motioned for me to follow him and I started to, but Ghostwalker made a noise that might have been clearing his throat and might have been a chuckle. "Voskovec? Don't forget your payment." He held out the envelope.

I took it. "You bet your spooky gray ass I won't forget this," I said.

Because now it was war. Bad enough he'd been screwing over Tina, but now Debbie was in his sights too. That made it personal. Hero or not, I made up my mind this bastard was going down. Hard.

One small consolation: when I got back to my car where I'd left it at Longmeadows, I took a minute to look at the envelope. There was actually twelve hundred in there, along with a note:

I added a little. It seemed like I owed you. I apologize for this. It wasn't my idea. I argued for payment in full. –A.

I shook my head. No matter what side of the street a guy was on, hero or villain, the bosses were jerks and the help tried their best to clean up after 'em. Some things were just universal, I guess.

◎◎◎

Nothing much happened for the next few days. Debbie and I were agreed that the girls could stay with us as long as they needed, and a couple of bugs I left at Tina's place showed me that Ghostwalker was leaving her be. As far as I could tell, he hadn't put it together that we knew each other. That suited me fine. Tina told me that the heist at Reichenbach wasn't supposed to go down for another week or so. The scheduling on it was very tight, she said, which suggested to me that whatever she was supposed to lift from there hadn't arrived yet.

That was okay by me, because it bought us a few days. I spent some time talking over possible plans with Tina, and more time talking to Trav about things he might have heard through his various contacts... and of course I was in my garage workshop a lot, putting together some things I thought would be useful. Meanwhile, my wife was in heaven entertaining Tina and Sarah, and she was even getting some color back. If it hadn't been for the threat of Ghostwalker hanging over everything it would have been almost like a fun family vacation or something.

After four days I was ready to put what I called Operation Payday into action. Tina had her part down, and I had checked in with Trav and made a couple of calls. All that was left was to pull the trigger on it.

"Tomorrow morning," I told Tina, and handed her the widget I'd been working on. "Hook it to your belt and leave it there. If it's not touching you somewhere it won't work. Leave the rest of it to me." I raised an eyebrow. "Sure you're up for this?"

Tina's eyes were hard. She nodded once. "More than you would ever believe." Normally you would never connect nice little Tina Jankewicz with Serpentina, but when she got that expression you could tell.

"Okay. Tomorrow, then. The old outfit's not too tight on you, is it?"

That got a big laugh. "You watch and see, old man. I've still got the moves."

◎◎◎

The Dain Pharmaceuticals corporate headquarters was in midtown, one of the new steel-and-glass monstrosities that had been sprouting in St. Jacques like mushrooms the last five years or so. I went in the main lobby, wearing my work coverall and gloves, with the goggles loose around my neck. I hadn't bothered with the tool belt; the stuff I would need was small enough to fit in my pocket.

Spoofing the executive elevator was easy enough with my bypass magnet—well, that's what I called it, little thing shaped kinda like a tuning fork, we can skip the *Popular Mechanics* lecture on how it worked. I hit the button for the penthouse level and when the doors whooshed open, there was a huge reception area with a little blue-haired lady in butterfly horn-rims sitting behind a big desk with half a dozen phones scattered across the top. She blinked in confusion. "How did you—there's no appointment in my book…"

"He'll see me," I said, and breezed in past her through the double doors.

I thought the blue-haired lady's desk in the reception area was big but the one Christopher Dain was sitting behind was twice its size, a glass-topped mahogany monster with enough surface area to serve as a helicopter pad. Dain was sitting and scowling at a file folder. Behind him was a floor-to-ceiling window that gave him the whole city as a backdrop. He looked up at me and his eyes widened in shock. He sputtered a little, but no words came out.

"Hey there, spookshow," I said.

For a second it looked like he might try and bluff it out, but then he just shrugged. "Voskovec." His voice was quiet and controlled but his face wore an expression of murderous anger. I think it was only the open doors behind me and the presence of the receptionist that kept him from trying to kill me with his bare hands. Instead he stood up slowly and walked around me to close the office doors. Then he returned to his desk and sat, glaring. Finally he said, "How did you find me? We took every precaution..."

"You keep making the same mistake." I shook my head. "I'm not some punk robber you gassed with fear juice. I'm a pro. I've been working with seriously scary people for years. You took precautions? I took precautions too. Took me a little while to work out millionaire industrialist Chris Dain was the big bad boo boy, but I had it figured a couple weeks ago." I pulled a little silver disk out of my pocket. "First night I was here, I put one just like this on the bottom of your phone downstairs—you know, the basement headquarters you have under this building where we been working the last few weeks. It scrambles any call I might make, it's rigged to recognize the particular frequency of my voice, but it's also got a record-and-transmit function. Gave me access to your whole network here."

"But we sweep for bugs! Every day!"

I rolled my eyes. "I keep telling you but you don't listen. This is my business, it's my *job* to outthink hero types like you. The guys what ask me to bug a place, they don't want the bug found. I originally whipped this up for Devilhound, it only transmits twice a day in a coded burst, maybe thirty seconds total. If you ain't doing your sweep during the minute or so it's active, the rest of the time it's just a tiny hunk of dead metal, no transmission to detect. Just a little voice-activated recorder. The only hard part's making it small enough to hide. Nobody on this side of the pond has it but the Russkies been using one like it for a couple of years now. Surprised your KGB buddies didn't supply you. But I guess they were holding out till you actually infiltrated the Liberty Brigade."

That rocked him, hard. I knew it would.

For a minute he was silent. Then he said slowly, "You didn't get that from a phone bug."

"No. I got it from using the smarts and the experience you hired me for. That fear gas gimmick you use, that couldn't have been Alistair. He built the delivery system, the thing in the gloves, but he's not a chemist. So it came from somewhere else. He probably thought the nerve agent was something one of your pharmaceutical employees here stumbled across, but he's not plugged in to the black market the bad guys use. I am, though. I tagged it as KGB stuff from the first night. The only question was where it came from." I grinned at him. "Your trouble is you think the villains are the be-all and end-all. You don't realize they all got support staff, brokers, whatever. None of you hero types ever figure out that the villain's crew hardly ever goes to jail because even a first-year public defender knows he can cut a deal for a henchman who spills on his boss, especially if some masked avenger in a leotard just beat the hell out of him and dropped him off at a police station." I spread my hands. "You and all the other caped crusaders don't think of us at all, but we ain't just background extras in some movie you're making in your head about good versus evil. We're a *community*, we talk to each other. All it took was a couple of calls to the right people to find out we had KGB agents in town. One of 'em has a little side hustle selling his secret-agent widgets and other things to the local masked-villain crowd. He's chatty if he thinks you're in the business and might be a new customer. My broker got a lot out of him." I paused. "But that guy's not your supplier. No, you get yours direct from Mother Russia, the KGB recruited you. I wonder how?"

Dain had murder in his eyes again. "What do you want?"

"I want my money and I want you to lay off Tina. Your deal with her is off. Your bosses will have to find out some other way if this thing Reichenbach's working on for the military is as good as what KGB has in the works. It's over for you."

Dain's laugh held no humor in it at all, just a sneer. "Seriously? What in the world makes you think I would do that? For that matter, don't you realize you'll never leave this building alive? You've overplayed your hand, Voskovec. You and your wife…"

"That's why I decided to you had to go down. Mess with my friends and family, I take that real personal. You shoulda' just paid me."

"You're no threat to me." Dain chuckled. "You were a fool to come here alone."

"Yeah. About that." I pulled the control box out of my pocket and flipped the switch. "I didn't."

On my right, Serpentina flickered into view, and on my left, Gravedigger did the same. I grinned at Dain again. "Like I said back on that first night at the fountain. I been doing lightbending stuff since '58. I even figured out how to beat the shimmer." Then I looked at the kid and said, "Told you I could prove it. He's in with the Commies. Up to his neck."

But the kid wasn't looking at me. He reached up and tore off his mask and stared in bafflement at Dain. "But... good God... Chris, *why?* All the time training—all the work we did on the streets..."

"It's all about the Liberty Brigade," I told him. "Russia's wanted inside that outfit since the war. They want superpeople of their own. That's why your boy here created the Ghostwalker identity. To audition. You, the car, everything, it's all window dressing. He needed to look good enough they would come to *him*, he had to set himself apart from all the other hopefuls in tights what come to this town. That's why he had to muscle Tina here for the Reichenbach blueprint job, so if it went bad Ghostwalker wouldn't be implicated. There was no way he could explain industrial espionage to Liberty Jane and the rest of 'em. That was just a side thing anyway, his KGB handlers saying, 'oh, and while you're in town, you need to get us these cutting-edge tech blueprints,' like asking somebody to pick up a quart of milk on the way home. He didn't dare endanger his real mission, to infiltrate the Liberty Brigade. That's why he suckered you into his costume gig in the first place, the Brigade's got a soft spot for teen sidekicks. Liberty Jane had Torchlight, Sergeant Smasher had Red Eagle, there was others. Nobody'd suspect Ghostwalker of being KGB if he had somebody like you next to him, all bright-eyed and ready to go do some capital-J Justice. Plus it kept you close at hand and loyal to him so when you turn twenty-one he can get his paws on your trust fund. He's playing all the angles. It's what rich assholes do."

"Robbie, don't listen to him. You know me, you know who I am." Dain sounded a little desperate now.

"I thought I did," the kid said. "But I guess I was just a naïve idiot." He looked at me. "But why did Alastair go along with it? I've known him my whole life. He would never..."

"You'd have to ask him," I said. "The spook must have something on him, same way he did Tina and me. That's all this creep knows how to do, find people's vulnerable spots and squeeze. Al wouldn't tell me what it was but he might tell you, especially now we've taken away Dain's leverage." I waved the disk at Dain, whose face was blotchy now with suppressed fury. "You have fifteen minutes to get a certified check for ten grand up here or a burst transmission of everything we've said in this office goes to the Brigade and the FBI." I paused and added, "You know what? Make it fifteen. I had more trouble over collecting from you than I did building the damn car. You can afford a bonus."

"You cheap crook," Dain gritted.

"I'm an *expensive* crook." I shrugged. "Warned you when we met this was going to run you some money."

Serpentina leaned forward. She held up her hand and clenched it into a fist. An eight-inch blade slid out of the wrist gauntlet. "Skip to the end, Chris. Make the call. Pay him. Or I'll slit your throat right here and now."

I could tell she wasn't kidding and I guess Dain could too, because he punched a button on his desk. "Renata, I need you to run down to Accounting and cut a check to Ernest Voskovec. V-O-S-K-O-V-E-C, yes, just like it sounds. Have one of the girls in the pool take it to the bank and have it certified. Put a rush on it. Fifteen minutes." He looked up at us. "Satisfied?"

"Almost," Serpentina cut in before I could say anything. Suddenly she leaped forward and did a tumbling flip across the desk to land right behind Dain, the blade at his throat. "Now that Ernie's been taken care of I want *my* fee," she hissed. "Your blackmailing women into bed is over with. I'm going to cut your manhood off. You're never going to force a woman again. Even that's too good for you."

Damn it. I knew there was more to it with the two of them than Tina told me but I hadn't put it all the way together.

Gravedigger—Robbie—was ashen. "Chris, you didn't...."

"Of course he did," I snapped. "Guys like him think they can do anything. It's why he wouldn't let you go with him when he went after her. But Tina, you can't—he's not worth it—think of Sarah, for Chrissake. You're better than him."

"She's just a whore in a snake suit," Dain snarled. His expression was the kind of savage desperation you see on a cornered animal, which is what he was now.

I guess he figured he had nothing left to lose. And seeing him in civvies, we kinda forgot that he was still, y'know, Ghostwalker. He wasn't just gimmicks, he had training—serious combat training, probably, way more than your usual spandex case. He was KGB now; never mind what he started as.

Anyway, he spun around all of a sudden, chopping away Serpentina's knife hand and then both she and him were moving too fast to follow, a flurry of chops and kicks and such that almost didn't look like fighting, but more like some kind of speeded-up dance routine. Serpentina still had the knife out but Dain suddenly had a blade too, I don't know if it was a letter opener in his desk or if he already had it on him, they were so quick I couldn't see. He had the advantage because of his size; he had a longer reach. Serpentina was holding her own but he was backing her up into the space between the desk and the window, and then she wasn't going to have room to duck and weave and kick like they'd been doing.

But Serpentina knew it too, and she snatched up the desk chair and threw it against the window. The glass shattered. The main patio was a ways off to the left; the penthouse window was just a couple feet from the edge of the roof. She leaped out on to the balcony rail outside. I thought for a second she was going to fall, but Tina hadn't been kidding when she said she still had the moves. "Let's dance, you son of a bitch. See if you can deal with a woman who's not scared of you." She brandished the blade with one hand and beckoned him with the other. "If you're man enough." Then she laughed and jumped off the roof. I thought for a second she was suicidal but then I saw her catch hold of a power line and spin, then she let go and sailed in a high arc up and over to the next building's roof. She was Olympic material, I'm telling you.

Dain was after her in seconds, peeling off his jacket and shirt to reveal the Ghostwalker outfit beneath. A lot of the costume guys did that, wore the outfit under their civilian clothes. Never understood it myself. I'd think you'd get really overheated.

All this takes a long time to tell but it was less than a minute between when Serpentina jumped on the desk and the time the two of them were leaping and backflipping across the rooftops.

"We have to stop them!" Robbie said. "Somebody's going to get killed!"

For a second I was going to say *what the hell d'you expect us to do?* And then I had an idea. "The *car*, kid, did Al finish the installation on the car? Is it ready?"

"I think so, he was having me help him with the wiring..."

"And the doors? He do up the exit like we were gonna do?"

"I don't know... I haven't seen him since..."

"We have to chance it, I guess." I pulled a little radio out of my pocket and thumbed the mic switch. "Atomic batteries to power! Turbines to speed! Hover mode, auto-home this signal, ignition and execute!"

Robbie blinked at me. "You kept one of our radios?"

"Precautions." I grinned at him. "This ain't my first rodeo, kid. You checked out on the car yet?"

Robbie looked a little sheepish. "Chris said there'd be time enough later."

"Figures." I sighed. "I guess I'm driving, then."

"But don't we have to go down to,,," Robbie's question was cut off by a whooshing roar as the cloud-gray Ghostmobile suddenly appeared outside the shattered window, all the hoverjets firing.

The kid gaped at me. "It flies? You and Alaistair built a *flying car?*"

"Been thinking about it for years," I waved at him to follow me. "Natural extension of the hovercraft design. Al did the math and I worked out the turbine stuff. Between us we figured out a way for us to actually get this thing in the air. But it's not very maneuverable up here and it maxes out the batteries, we gotta move quick. I don't know how much charge it's got. We might only have a few minutes." I hit the button on the radio to open the roof hatch and tried not to think about what would happen if I missed a step. It was a long way down.

When I was behind the wheel I felt better. After the kid was safe in the passenger seat I closed the hatch. A bunch of screens came alive. I said, "Auto-home Ghostwalker, execute," and we were off. So far everything was working like it was supposed to. I'd have been feeling smug if I wasn't so worried about Tina. As it was I was just trying to figure out some way for all of us to get out of this alive. Damn headstrong girl, she was going to blow everything.

We caught up with them in a minute or so, they'd only made it a couple of blocks. They were still fighting. Ghostwalker had shucked the rest of his civvies and was masked up now, and he and Serpentina were trading blows on the roof of a parking garage, bouncing all over the place. Over and through and around the parked cars like some kind of urban obstacle course. Once again he was using his size advantage to press her toward the edge. If she went over, it was twelve stories down and nothing to grab hold of.

"There's no place to set down," Robbie said. "We're too big..."

"I don't want to set down." I looked at the array of buttons and switches. "Did Al get the cable gun in..."

We were still about thirty yards out from the roof of the garage. Ghostwalker got in a punch that sent Serpentina reeling to the edge of the roof. And he followed it up with a kick that knocked her all the way over.

No time to think. Al had got it done or he hadn't. Nothing was labeled yet but I knew where the button was. I hit it and a harpoon shot out trailing the cable I'd picked up last week, thudding into the side of the parking structure a couple of stories down from the roof. Still falling, Serpentina twisted in mid-air and caught it with one hand, and I backed up slow so the cable'd be taut. She reached up with her other hand and pulled herself up so she was kinda sitting on it.

Ghostwalker wasn't done. He dived off the roof, trying for the cable, but something went wrong. He didn't have his glider-cape-jacket and that might have made the difference. Or he just misjudged it. Tina swore later that she hadn't shook the cable and maybe she didn't, but for whatever reason he missed, falling the rest of the way to the street. Nine stories. He didn't even scream.

I opened the roof hatch. "Get out there and help her, we got maybe five minutes before this place is swarming with cops and ambulances and maybe even Brigade. Now, kid!"

Robbie was in shock, I think, but my barking at him brought him out of it. He nodded and climbed up and out to help Serpentina, who was coming hand-over-hand up the cable to us. She grabbed on to him and both of them plopped into the passenger seat, her on his lap. It was awkward and cramped but it was good enough. I punched another button to release the cable and said, "Auto-home, garage." We sailed up and away.

I looked at the two of them and sighed. "This is going to go bad very fast once they pull that mask off his body. And KGB might have a cleanup crew ready to clear Dain's building of anything implicating them. We don't got time for post-mortems. Kid, you and Al are gonna have to get whatever you need out of the workshop before someone else gets to it. Tina, you get changed and head for home, I think it's safe now. Dain wouldn't have told the Russians about you."

"What about Sarah?" Tina pulled off her hood and looked at me with wide scared eyes. It was all starting to sink in.

"Debbie and I will bring her by in a while." I grinned. "After I pick up my check."

◎◎◎

Ernie Voskovec set the sheaf of papers down and whistled. "Wow. That was… something."

"Is it okay?" Christine couldn't help feeling anxious.

"It's better than okay." Ernie shook his head. "I mean, it's all there like I told you but you made it… it reads like a story. I could never do that."

"I just cleaned it up a little," Christine said, blushing. "I'm glad you like it. I did have questions," she added.

"Sure. Shoot."

"What happened with Alastair?"

Voskovec snorted. "Well, it got hushed up about Dain pretty quick, KGB knew when to cut their losses. Nobody really wanted to go there, not the cops nor the corporate folks on the Dain Pharmaceuticals board. Money's a superpower all its own, you know. And then Liberty Jane got into it, so it all got worked out pretty quick. You probably know Ghostwalker did end up in the Brigade. Was a full member till they broke up in '81 or whenever it was."

"But it was Robbie."

"Yeah." Voskovec grinned. "There's lots of high-minded talk about justice and public service and so on with them hero guys but the truth is, folks what get into the life, they get hooked on it. Robbie didn't want to quit and he talked Al around. After all, they had all the equipment and everything. And Dain had played it close enough to the vest that neither the cops nor the KGB found the underground garage. They operated out of there till the Brigade signed 'em up."

"And Tina?"

Now it was Voskovec who was flushing. "Well, I split my check with her. Seemed only fair. Gave her a fresh start. She and Sarah landed out in Arizona. Tina coached college gymnastics out in Tempe till she retired. Sarah's in grad school, I think. She'd be about your age now. I forget the major, it's archaeology or something like that."

"You split the check with her." Christine raised an eyebrow. "After all that trauma to get it."

"Well, she helped a lot. And after what Dain did to her…"

Christine laughed. "You talk so tough, Ernie, but you have a good heart too. You're just a big softy."

Voskovec was still red, but he grinned at that. He shrugged. "Maybe. But don't let it get out, toots. I got a rep."

THE END

AFTERWORD: CAR TALK

I've always loved Big Science in adventure fiction. Got hooked on stuff like *Jonny Quest* and *Fantastic Four* when I was a kid and that led to Heinlein juveniles like *Have Space Suit Will Travel* and the Bantam Doc Savage paperbacks and, well, it's just always been a thing with me. So it's been a real treat to do my own variation on it with Dr. Fixit, handyman to the supervillain set.

I was telling my wife Julie, "See, Ernie's like Dr. Benton Quest if he'd had to drop out of high school to feed his family or something. Reed Richards, but working class. Played by Ernest Borgnine."

My bride snorted. "Who are you kidding? Ernie is **you.** He hates rich people pushing him around and he loves his wife. He gets into this because he's trying to get her medicine. It's so obvious."

Well, maybe. Your output is derived from your input. God knows we've spent way too much of the last year and a half dealing with insurance and health issues, and I admit it was a little cathartic to get some fictional payback against a pharmaceutical executive prone to changing the rules at whim. Plus it was a way to make a point I've been wanting to sneak into a story for years… idealist rich-guy heroes like Bruce Wayne and Richard Wentworth, they couldn't possibly exist. No one gets to be a millionaire without stepping on a few people, not even the inherited-wealth crew. It occurred to me that it would be fun to play with the idea of a gentleman-adventurer costumed hero who genuinely *was* the kind of jerk millionaire we see in real life, trampling underlings and taking credit from working-class employees who actually are doing the real labor.

And that made him the perfect adversary for Doc Fixit, blue-collar genius engineer. As recounted in *Mystery Men (and Women)* volume six, I had originally intended Ernie just as a one-off, but when Cap'n Ron asked for more, I suddenly saw a way to do sequels, and that led to me thinking of various cool things Ernie could build. His era's later than most of Airship 27's new-pulp heroes. Doc Fixit's heyday is the sixties, the Groovy Age: Bond, Batman, and bionics, the pulp adventures *I* grew up on. So of course the coolest vehicle ever, the Batmobile, was a natural springboard idea for a Doc Fixit project. (The 1966 Batmobile, that is, or as we say in our household, "the **real** one." There's a reason my author photo at Amazon is me sitting in that car.) The rest came from that.

There will be more Doc Fixit adventures to come. Each of these seems to lead to the next... Look for *Dr. Fixit's Island Getaway* in the not-too-distant future, the story of how Devilhound 'bought it' out in the South Pacific, and what *really* happened in the big showdown there with Cetacean. Further deponent sayeth not.

◉◉◉

GREG HATCHER - has been writing for one outlet or another since 1992. He was a contributing editor at WITH magazine for over a decade and during that time was a three-time winner of the Higher Goals Award for children's writing; once for fiction and twice for non-fiction. Following that he did a weekly column for Comic Book Resources as one of the rotating features on the Comics Should Be Good! blog for eleven years. Currently he is doing a weekly column on pop culture for Atomic Junk Shop. He also teaches writing in the Young Authors classes offered as part of the Communities In Schools Afterschool Arts Program in west Seattle, for students in the 6th through the 12th grade. A fan of pulp fiction ever since he discovered the Doc Savage paperback reprints from Bantam Books in the 1970s, he has contributed a number of action-adventure stories to various 'new pulp' anthologies in recent years. Likewise a lifelong mystery fan, he has also written Nero Wolfe pastiches for the Wolfe Pack Gazette and several Sherlock Holmes adventures for the Airship 27 CONSULTING DETECTIVE series. He lives in Burien, Washington, with his wife Julie, their cat Magdalene, and ten thousand books and comics.

THE GHOUL STRIKES!

By Harding McFadden and Eleanor Hawkins

M arvin "Ghoul" MacCormac slowed the car as he drew into the town proper, leaving the paved road behind and rolling onto the hard-packed dirt. The late Autumn night was crisp and silver, the skeletal full moon giving everything a phantasmal, funereal feel. Quinnstown looked dead.

Hours earlier he'd gotten a telegram from his camera girl, Marion Mc-Givern, telling him that something was up with this small, mostly farm-ridden burg. A week before he'd sent her to investigate some weird happenings that his mysterious benefactor had brought to his attention, things that bore looking into. Since then he'd heard not a word from the diminutive former spy. Then came her telegram.

Within a half dozen miles he knew were a few farms, none making more than a bare living, most on the verge or past it of financial ruin. Such were the times, that most of the farmers, their wives and children, had to look for ways to earn extra money. As Ghoul understood it, most found work in town, doing whatever they could to help out their own.

Driving through the center of the town proper, he peeled his eyes looking for any signs of life. It was well past midnight, and he knew that not a soul would be about, but having survived life in the city, and four years of Hell on earth in Europe, he'd learned to take nothing for granted. He had more scars than he cared to count from bullets, knives, and a fairly deep divet from a blackjack hidden beneath his hairline to let him know that it was the inattentive man that paid the piper first.

On both sides of the road were little shops, fronted by boardwalks or the first attempts at sidewalks. He could see a sewer's roost, a few restaurants, a mechanic's. At the end of the main street was a library, complete with wrought iron railings and stone lions at the bottom of its steps. Across from it was a self-important brick structure that could only be the township building. In the middle distance was the eye-catcher:

In her telegram, Marion had mentioned the large house, nearly a mansion that did its best to look like a dwarf castle. It was the center of the problems that were dropping down on Quinnstown like a fire from Heaven. She'd been subtle in her wording, no doubt unwilling to give the locals the impression that she was worried. But for someone who'd known her for a long while, as he'd known her for nearly twenty years, her words were signal flares. Something was happening here. And it was happening tonight.

Drifting the car to the thin concrete curb in front of the library, under one of the half dozen lampposts spread out down the street, he shut off the engine and sat for a quiet minute, listening. The wind was harsh, not enough to rock the car, but rattling the nearby trees with ease. Throwing up the heavy collar of his black trench coat, he took his hat from the seat next to him and exited the car.

The car door shut with a pistol crack that echoed into the night, carried along the wind like it was the pied piper. If anyone was awake within a mile of him, he had no doubt they'd heard it.

His breath coming out of him in thin puffs, he walked to the center of the street and looked around. Something was wrong, he thought. He was being watched.

Not for the first time, he was glad of the twin thin automatics holstered under his armpits.

Walking across the street, he ascended the steps to the front doors of the township building. Trying them and finding them locked, he grunted. Not surprising, but frustrating nevertheless. Scanning the street again, sure he was not alone, he held his breath, squinted his eyes into the moonlit night, and saw his company.

A hundred yards away, in the direction from which he'd entered town, he could just make out the shambling, running sight of a man, making his quick way toward Ghoul. The way he moved, the fellow was either drunk or hurt. More than once he fell, only to rocket back up and keep up his advance.

When he was at last about a dozen feet from the township building, the stranger let out a snarling shriek like a wounded animal and threw himself wholeheartedly into an end run that brought him to the foot of the steps in three mammoth leaps.

Pulling the .45 from under his left arm, Ghoul aimed it at the stranger, and in a voice that left no room for discussion, demanded, "Stay where you are."

Still shrieking, the stranger lunged up the steps, hands like claws, murder in his intent. In the moments before he pulled the trigger, Ghoul got his first good look at the man.

The fellow was hardly the Ghoul's own age, just forty, but looked worse. His skin was the color of old milk, the bags under his eyes heavy and drooping. His mouth was dry and chapped; his teeth loose and black, the gums pulled back severely. He was emaciated to the point that his executioner wondered how he was able to move at all. His clothes were tattered and threadbare, covered here and there with every imaginable manner of filth, and not a little blood. His feet were bare, bruised, and bleeding.

With a decisive *crack!* the .45 went off, the 230 grain slug slamming into the monstrous man like a hammer, launching him back down the steps, to land on the sidewalk with a sickening splat.

Standing at the top of the flight, looking down at his would-be attacker, Ghoul twitched when he heard new sounds, now. More moans and animal screams, seemingly coming from all around him!

◎◎◎

Slipping a pair of well-worn leather gloves from his trench coat pocket, Ghoul stooped to look at his fallen attacker. Wary that the man might yet have some fight left in him, he was cautious as he looked through his pockets, searching for anything to tell him just who this madman might have been.

Coming up empty, always aware of the shrieks coming ever closer to him in the enclosing night, he turned his examination to the man's body. Ripping open the fellow's shirt, Ghoul saw masses of bruises, purple and rotten green; under these he could detect, even in the silver light of the moon, that the muscles were bunched, flexed and contorted painfully, explaining just why the man's movements had been so erratic.

Looking at the attacker's hands, Ghoul was made uneasy by the filth and flesh gummed under the nails, as though the man had been in a life and death struggle, fought like an animal, ripping and rending to stay alive, and had not bothered to clean the grisly evidence from his person afterword. The veins at the top of the hand stood out, like those of a much older man nearing the end of his life, not like those of someone only entering his forth decade upon this world.

Growing concerned, an inkling of what he was looking at entering his razor sharp mind, Ghoul pulled his hands quickly from the dead man, and looked him over with growing alarm. Lunging at the dead man's face, he quickly lifted his hooded eyelids, seeing the massive red, vine-like coloring on the eyes. With a thumb, cautious of the teeth, he pulled up the body's upper lip and saw the flecks of foam at the corners of the mouth and welling at the back of the throat, settling down in death.

Standing and taking a few quick steps back from the body; Ghoul pulled his gloves off and threw them on top of the corpse. A smart man, with more than his share of combat medical experience—as both caregiver and patient—he was nevertheless not a doctor. At best he could only guess, but felt for certain that what he was looking at was rabies, though like none that he had ever seen before.

Suddenly aware of how exposed he was there, he turned to run toward his waiting auto. His mind was a blur of thought, pieces of a much larger puzzle falling into place, their implications something he'd rather not think about until he'd had time to process.

Closer now than he'd have thought possible, the screams and moans that lived and bred in the night sent a cold chill running up his spine. In spite of himself his hair stood on end.

The dead man, his body wracked with rabies, had come at him intent on murder or spreading the disease which was even then killing him. This the Ghoul understood. It was the way this sickness worked, forcing itself in all directions; taking over the world one bite or scratch at a time.

One rabies-ridden man in an area he could understand. While unfortunate, these things did happen. More than one? The numbers that the sounds rushing up at him implied? It was unheard of. And to have worked so quickly?

Marion McGivern had contacted him only hours ago, and if there were this kind of outbreak in Quinnsville, she surely would have at least made mention of it, on her way out of town no doubt. But she'd written nothing of it. Which could only mean that what was happening was more recent than should have been possible. A potentially population-wide scourge of rabies in only a few hours!

Only a few feet from the comparative safety of his car, Ghoul recognized the sounds of running feet coming at him from his right. Slim pistol instantly in his hand, he turned in time to see a woman lunging at him. At one time undoubtedly attractive, she was now haggard and rabid, her eyes bright red and bulging, her body twitching and bending like millions of volts of electricity were running through her. Her lips were pulled back from long teeth, bubbling saliva running from her mouth like a fetid river. Clawed hands extended toward him, broken nails jagged and grimed, she screamed in the back of her throat, the bestial sound raising gooseflesh along his neck.

Squeezing off a quick shot, he saw her turn in midair, landing on the back of her head, still writhing, even while unable to stand. With more pity than malice, he put another slug through her head, silencing her once and for all.

In no time at all, the rest were upon him. From every direction they came, dozens of maddened men and women and, good Lord, even children! Like the unburied dead, they moved toward him in a wave of corrupted humanity, pushing over each other, grinding those slower souls beneath thundering heels. In seconds they would be upon him, and he knew that he didn't have enough bullets, or time, to take care of them all!

◉◉◉

Two more of the tormented souls were upon Ghoul in seconds, grabbing him and sending him crashing to the ground beside his auto. A woman and younger man, they pulled at him, ripping his hat from his head, crushing the wind from his lungs. With a grunt and a gasp, he shot the man under the chin, turning his head away in what he hoped wasn't a futile attempt to keep this disease from infiltrating his body. When he turned his attention to the woman, she was tearing at the heavy sleeve of his coat with her teeth, gnawing like a dog on a bone, growling in her throat. Shoving the still-warm barrel of the pistol against her bulging right eye, he squeezed the trigger, and relieved her of her torment.

From behind and around the car, he saw more of the possessed horde coming his way. Always a decisive man, he abandoned the car, putting as many steps between himself and his rabid attackers as he could. Beating feet up the steps of the township building, he collided with the locked double doors at the top, slamming them open with a sound of shattering wood and rending steel.

Making a quick turn, he shoved the doors closed again, dragging a heavy waiting couch against them to slow, however briefly, his attackers. Starting down a long hallway toward the back of the building, he was pulled up short by the sounds of shattering glass and moaning cries there that reached his ears from back there. They were entering the building!

Turning around, he bounded up a flight of steps toward the second floor of the building as the first of his pursuers made it through the couch barricade, meeting up with their fellow madmen from the back of the building in a perfect storm of fury and foaming insanity. Taking the steps two at a time, he prayed that he wouldn't stumble and fall. To do so would be the end of him, and he couldn't think of many worse ways to go.

Hitting the landing at the top of the flight of steps, he quickly ascended a third, the insane townspeople hardly five feet behind. At the end of this final hallway was a large window, floor to ceiling and six feet wide, with a wonderful view of a streetlight perhaps six feet from it. At a full run, the shrieks and wails ever closer, the moist, wet breath of his attackers heavy on his neck, Ghoul charged up the hall.

Coat dropped to the floor behind him as he ran, he shielded his face with his arms and burst through the window, raining glass in the street below and peppering his hair and clothes with glittering fragments. He grunted as numerous cuts and scrapes opened up on his face and head despite his best efforts to shield them, and was keenly aware of a long gash on his right forearm that he could feel already beginning to saturate his shirt with warm blood.

Arms instantly outstretched, he grabbed at the lamppost and held on for dear life as the beasts that had pursued followed him out the window, only to crash to the street below in a series of wet cracks and pops. Swinging wildly in the air, he nearly fell as one of the mad horde, a blonde haired man with farmer's arms, managed to jump a bit further than the others, his fingertips making contact with Ghoul's left shoe, pulling it off as he fell to the ground.

Pulling himself up onto the curved top of the lamppost, Ghoul surveyed the scene around him. At the window were a dozen or more of the rabid attackers, each shrieking at him, their exposed teeth gnashing in his direction, his distance tormenting them unbelievably. On the ground were only the damaged and dead, most still, others twitching and convulsing, their bodies twisted in ways that only a broken back could explain.

Grabbing onto the lamppost with both arms and legs, he quickly shimmied down to street level, took his stolen shoe from the gibbering man who'd taken it from him, and ran again for his car. Once he was inside, he turned over his engine, and was just beginning to roll when the first of the remaining attackers reached him, slamming into his auto like a subhuman tidal wave. The car rocked on its wheels as he shifted gears and accelerated at full speed away from there. Along the way he drove over more than one of the monstrous citizens of Quinnsville, crushing them to pulp beneath his spinning rubber tires.

◎◎◎

The wheels kicked up bits of rock and other debris as he burned his way down the dirt road out of town, looking in his rearview mirrors only to be sure that none of the demonic denizens were hanging from the car. The distance between the horde and himself grew with each passing second. At first so close to him that he could see their bloodshot eyes perfectly, could practically feel their fetid breath on the back of his neck, they were presently a dozen yards behind; fifty yards; a hundred.

Like a silent picture, their howling visages were unaccompanied by sound, their tortured wails blocked by his roaring engine, and the road swiftly passing beneath him.

After a couple of minutes, his tires hit blacktop with a thud, and he spun his wheel to the right, skidding loudly back onto the road toward civilization. The nearest regular town was a full forty miles away, and even at top speed would take the better part of an hour.

Another few minutes, and a few miles, from Quinnsville, he passed a glass-housed payphone. Slamming on his breaks, he put the car in park, leaving it running in case the sickness had spread further than he figured it had, and got out. Thumbing his coins into the slot, he listened impatiently for any sign that the operator knew he was on the line. He needed to get a call through to Boston, to his man in the news, Ira Grimm. Needed to get the word out about what was happening here in this little corner of No-where, Pennsylvania. Before it spread. Before it enveloped the world.

Striking the phone after more than a full minute without contact with the operator, he clenched his eyes and forced himself to calm down, to think logically. He returned the phone to its dead cradle. Something was happening here, and Marion McGivern had warned him. Some kind of manmade evil, situated in that pretentious dwarf castle he'd seen in the dis-tance. Apparently the phones near town were goners. Why? To stop word from getting out until it was too late?

Exiting the booth, he stood in the center of the street, in exactly the same way he had back in town. He listened. The wind was picking up, the chill deepening, but he didn't figure on rain. When it rained, he was always warned, by aches and pains in every place he'd ever broken. That made for a lot of aches and pains. There were no other signs of life. The town was isolated, perfectly alone. A farming community, with few or no contacts with the outside world. An incubator. A closed environment, readymade for whatever evil plots the inhabitants of the castle had in mind.

He had to go back. He knew it, but didn't have to like it. Things were going on there that would undoubtedly have repercussions in the world at large. People were dead or dying at the whim of some madman or group of madmen. Add to that Marion McGivern, his friend and companion and fellow traveler of many years, was there, and the choice was really no choice at all.

He returned to the car and popped open the glove box and took out a box of ammunition. Removing the magazine from the pistol that he'd fired quite a few times into the rabid townsfolk, he topped it off from the box, then removed a few empty magazines from the glovebox and filled them as well. Slipping a few of the mags in slots in his shoulder holsters, he dropped the rest in his pants pockets, with a few loose spares for good measure.

With a grunt of frustration and not a little determination, he got back behind the wheel and did a quick U-turn, heading back toward town, to-ward Marion, and whatever evil fate had waiting for him.

◉◉◉

About a mile short of town he killed the engine and let the car roll to a quiet halt against the side of the road. Breath coming in slow gulps, he extended his concentration to its utmost, and listened, truly *listened*, to the distant sounds of Armageddon.

From the low moans drifting to him over the increasing winds, he estimated that the town's folk were a good distance off, no doubt following some new prey, real or imagined. More's the better. As long as they were well off over there, he might just have the time to learn what he needed to know.

Exiting the car, he closed the door gingerly, making no sound at all. For a long minute he stood there, hand hovering over the grip of a pistol, waiting to defend himself, life and limb, against the poor souls that had fallen under the Evil machinations of the owner of the castle. After a time, with nothing to show for his patience, he made his slow way onward.

He made his way in good time, not daring to run, making his footsteps as like the falling leaves of mid-Autumn. He was a shadow in shadows, something that had saved his life countless times before.

At the corner of a building, when he at last had made his methodical way into the town, only a few dozen yards from where he'd been assaulted near his car, he made himself as invisible as he was able. He thought transparent thoughts. Strain his eyes as he might, taking darting glimpses around the corner, down the length of the main street. He could see no inhabitant, other than those broken bodies that he'd left in his wake hardly an hour earlier. He thanked God that at least their moans and cries of anguish had stopped. They'd shuffled off, into whatever restful rewards or punishments awaited them in the world beyond this one.

Still hugging the wall, he drew a pistol and started his way up the street slowly. Whenever the opportunity presented itself, he worked between buildings, living in the deeper darkness gathered there, birthed by nightfall and clicking overhead streetlights. His breath was plumed in cottony puffs as the night grew colder, forcing him to pull a large handkerchief from his back pocket and tie it around his lower face. The puffs somewhat more dispersed, he was nevertheless aware of how the sounds of his breathing were all the louder for his effort to hide their escape.

At the base of the stairs that led to the desiccated doors of the township building, he stood silent for another long moment, listening, needing to be sure that none of those who'd entered in pursuit of him were still inside. Better to not find himself locked in with killers more than once tonight.

Hearing no sounds coming from inside, he quick-footed it up the steps, into the building, and the warm darkness within.

◉◉◉

Step by anxious step, he ascended the stairs to the upper floors of the building, noticing black stains here and there where his earlier pursuers had trampled each other into bloody messes in their haste to get him. With quick copper flashes of a penlight, he looked at the signs painted on the opaque glass at the top of each door, looking for anything that might give him a clue about deeds. At the farthest end of the hall from the head of the stairs he saw a pretentious banner that read *T. Wolfe, City Planner.*

With a quick shove of his shoulder, he forced the door, and entered the room, again stopping to listen to the silence. When nothing reached his ears, he let out a slow breath and began to search the wall of filing cabinets that took up nearly half the room, the other space being occupied by a too-large desk, fronted by disproportionately small chairs, no doubt meant to leave visitors feeling small in the presence of such a great man as this T. Wolf, City Planner.

After more than an hour of careful searching, he could find no mention anywhere of the castle, nor its nefarious occupant. For all the world it was like they didn't exist. Or, perhaps, he thought, turning to look over the room, they were just too important to be put in with all the little people.

Taking a seat behind the large desk, he began pulling out drawers, feeling in his bones that what he was looking for was here. The two sets of over-under drawers to either side of the desk were unlocked and filled with pads of papers, names and addresses of important locals, and other useless brickabrack. The center drawer, shorter than the others and situated at naval-level, was locked. Forcing it was the work of seconds.

Inside was a revolver, unloaded with a handful of shells next to it, a picture of a later-middle aged man—bearded, balding, glasses: Wolfe?—with a big-haired blonde woman young enough to be his daughter, but obviously not, and a thick folder, unmarked, full of papers.

Leaving the picture and the revolver, he removed the folder and flipped through its contents. Bingo!

The deed to the castle, all important documentation, and a name: Napoleon Chort. In flowery longhand, he read Wolf's brief notes about meeting with this Chort, his feelings of unease, as if of all the shady people that he'd dealt with in his less than reputable life had been but fakes and amateurs, nothing compared to the actual threat of a horrifyingly dangerous and deadly monster like Napoleon Chort.

Under the note and deed to the castle, there set a stack of smaller file folders, each with a different name typed on a corner, with a country accompanying. The first read James Balor-Ireland. Flipping through it, Ghoul

Forcing the locked drawer was the work of seconds.

was aghast at the list of atrocities associated with this Balor, murder, torture, horrific brainwashing. Whoever this Balor was, he was only human in the strictest meaning of the word. Even animals didn't treat their kin in such manner.

Beneath the Balor file were more, each recounting more of the same: Dioval-Romania; Shentani-Africa; Appolyon-Greece. It wasn't until he got to the last file in the stack that Ghoul's breath stopped short. His body broke out in a cold sweat, his disbelieving eyes locked on the name of the devil: Teufel-Germany.

With shaking fingers he flipped through the file, the most recent of the stack, reliving their contents for the first time in more than a decade. He looked at the atrocities committed by the Butcher of Berlin, atrocities that he'd seen firsthand in his time in Europe. The wholesale slaughter he'd seen there, the body-strewn boneyards of No Man's Land, the field hospitals where he'd seen the best of men stitched back together from too few parts, himself included, had all paled in comparison to the things that he's seen done at the hands of Teufel.

Centered in this last file was a picture, the cold demon's eyes unmistakable. He'd seen them before and been chilled to the bone by them. But that had been years ago. The picture that he looked down at now was more recent, but unfocused, covert, lacking detail. The devil had aged since the old days, but it was nevertheless him. The Butcher. Teufel. Dioval. Appolyhon. Napoleon Chort.

He was here, in Quinnstown, continuing his work, alive and well and corrupting the very air of the place by simply having been here!

In anger, rage born of memory and pain, Ghoul hurled the thick bundle of files through the air, a snarling hiss escaping his clenched teeth. He was here. Over his horrible lifetime, the Butcher had traveled the world, doling out pain and misery at will, suffering no consequence for his reign of terror. But no more. It stopped tonight.

He's here, Ghoul thought, his breath calming, his face setting in a terrifying rictus of determination. *He's here. But so am I...*

◉◉◉

In the silence that filled the room, Ghoul suddenly became aware of a whispered shudder, hardly heard. Instantly alert, brought back to his senses by a need to survive, to avenge countless lives lost at the hands of The Butcher, he squinted into the dark and observed the room.

He had little doubt that the sounds he heard were not from one of the tortured inhabitants of this place. Had they heard his ruckus, they'd have come on in a fury, snarling and grabbing, with no thought of concealing their presence.

Making hardly a sound, he rounded the desk and made his way to the center of the room. Reluctantly, he closed his eyes and stood listening, letting his ears adjust to the room. Instantly he located the source of the whispered breathing.

Gun at the ready, he gripped the knob of the room's only closet, and yanked open the door. It swung open silently on well-oiled hinges. Within he saw only the barest of outlines, a silhouette concealed by shadow.

Holding a silencing finger to his lips, he used his gun hand to beckon the stranger out. Reluctantly, she left the deeper shadows, emerging into the room.

Under more ideal circumstances, he could have seen how some would have found her attractive. Pleasantly shaped, with a bob of lustrous blonde hair and intense blue eyes, she was nevertheless barely an adult, and though there was certainly no reason to complain about her look or figure, he had to admit that she'd had better days. Her face was pale and drawn, her makeup running and dry to her cheeks. Her dress was rumpled, and though hardly expensive, looked decidedly the worse for wear.

"What's your name?" Ghoul asked, lowering his pistol but not re-holstering it.

Voice like a whispered breeze, she replied, "Marlene. Marlene Moore."

Nodding, he said, "Ok, Marlene, why don't you come in here and tell me what the devil's going on?"

Hugging herself, she moved further into the room, perching herself on the corner of the large desk while Ghoul silently moved one of the guest chairs to wedge it under the knob of the main door. With the glass top to the door, the gesture was useless, but it at least gave him the feeling of accomplishing something. In a worse situation, it might buy them the tenth of a second that would make all the difference.

Standing before her, he placed his free hand upon her shoulder and asked, "Now tell me: what's happened here?"

She rocked slightly, her eyes glassy and unfocused. "I was in the basement, taking my lunch," she started. A frown creased her face. "That was the only place to get away from Mr. Wolf. My boss. I've had worse bosses. I mean, he didn't shout at me or hit me or anything, but he was always just so... Gross towards me. Always looking at me like I was on a menu, y'know. I didn't want to be alone with him, but work being what it is right now, I couldn't just quit, either. I think he knew that. He'd started getting touchy lately, so I started eating in the basement.

"I was down there, reading, and I must have fallen asleep. All of a sudden, I start hearing this screaming, like nothing I'd ever heard. I had an uncle who lost a hand and two fingers in a thresher when I was a kid, and it was a little like that, but about a hundred times worse. It was like everybody'd been caught in that thresher.

"I could hear them shouting, and running around up there, and things getting thrown around or knocked over. Ain't afraid to admit it: I was scared sick. I ran over to the door and locked it right up. We don't use the basement except for storage, but it was built for things that shouldn't just get out—deeds and such—so the door was solid, and the locks good.

"I'd no more'n locked that door when I heard these heavy feet come slammin' down the steps, and someone run full force into it. I was so scared I couldn't even cry. I just crawled into a corner and hid there like a mouse." She shuddered, eyes clenched shut tight. Thin tears ran down her pale cheeks. "Seemed like that banging went on forever. Every time, I figured the door'd pop right off its hinges, and I'd get ate up by whatever was out there. 'Cept, I knew what it was: Mr. Wolf. Don't ask me how I knew, but I just did, and I knew that he'd come runnin' because he knew I'd be there.

"A long while went by, and the banging slowed down, then stopped altogether. I sat in that corner for hours. Couldn't make myself move. Got to feeling lightheaded, and got this pain in my chest was so bad, I thought I was havin' a heart attack. It was probably after dark when I could move again.

"Then all of a sudden I hear a big bang coming from upstairs. I figured someone'd kicked in the doors. We always lock them up when we close down to eat. Then more shouting, and running, and glass breaking."

Ghoul was nodding. "That'd be me," he said. "Got a very warm welcome when I showed up."

She looked at him wide-eyed. "You got away? Then why are you here? Why aren't you out getting help?"

He shook his head. "Hate to break this to you, Miss Moore, but I don't think there's anyone to get help for. The town's people—most all of them, near as I can tell—had something happen to 'em. They've all gone rabid. No help for 'em."

She was crying more heavily now, her body wracked with great sobs.

"I'm sorry to have to do this to you, miss, but I have something I need to know: A friend of mine was here, a lady. Little on the short side, fire engine red hair, with an eye patch. Y'seen her?"

Forcing composure, Marlene Moore nodded. "Small town," she answered. "Your friend kind of stands out."

Ghoul nodded again, a crooked half smile lifting one side of his grim mouth. *You don't know the half of it, lady.*

"Do you have any idea where she might be? Where was the last place you saw her?"

She was shaking her head sadly. "Oh, mister, I don't know. Last place I saw her was at the Domino—big black and white restaurant down the end of the block. But that was late last night or early this morning. She could be in China now for all I know."

Ghoul straightened. Well, that's decided, then. Either she was off causing mischief at the castle, or...

He set his brow. "All right, miss, here's the deal: I've got to go find my friend, or take care of those that've done for her. Your best bet is to get back in the basement, and lock yourself in good and tight."

She was standing, grabbing him by the collar, eyes wild with fear. "No no no, you can't leave me by myself. I'll go mad, I know I will. Mister, I'm barely holding on now as it is. Wherever it is you're goin', take me with you. I'd rather be in hell with company than in purgatory alone right now."

With a heavy sigh, he looked at her, then out of the office windows. It was getting colder. He still figured the snow and rain would hold off, but not the chill. The panes were frosting over, the world beyond silvered by the moon.

Reluctantly, he nodded. He'd regret it, he knew. But the chances of either of them getting out of this situation alive were slim to none as it was. Better to give the girl a chance to die on her feet, rather than cowering in a corner, like a terrified little mouse.

◉◉◉

Removing the revolver and shells from the presumably late Mr. Wolf's desk, Ghoul held them out to the woman and asked, "You know how to use one of these?"

She took the gun from him with obvious distaste, opened the cylinder, and started feeding the rounds into the holes. "Yeah," she answered with a sneer. "Everybody around here does. Don't much like them, though."

He turned from her and moved the chair from under the doorknob. "Doesn't matter," he told her. "Like 'em or not, more than likely if you live through tonight, it'll be because you had it in your hand. Don't forget it: you can't fight evil with just bad words and a chip on your shoulder. If you have to use it, use it. You'll have the rest of your life to come to terms with it."

Opening the door, he leaned out and looked down the dark hallway, seeing nothing. Strain his ears as he might, he could make out no other presence in the building. Didn't mean much, he knew; until he found her, he hadn't known Marlene was in the room with him.

Beckoning her to follow, he moved into the shadows and down the stairs. Every so often, he'd stand still and listen, but never heard a thing, other than her breathing on the step right above his.

The street was empty, except for those poor souls that he'd helped dispatch earlier in the evening. Looking at them from the darkness of the doorway, where they were sprawled out, broken and shattered under the streetlight, like some morbid stage show, he could detect no movement. Whatever thread of life they'd held to had snapped. They were gone, resting in a more comfortable place, he hoped, than the world of late had been for them.

"Stay close to the buildings," he told her. "No noise. You're not even here, understand?"

He could sense her nod.

They left the township building and made their way with as much stealth as they could muster toward the distant castle. With each step, the air seemed to grow thicker, charged with some kind of wretched current. The hellish power of the place, he knew. He'd felt it before, in the War, when he'd been elbows deep in the worst than humanity had to offer.

When they heard the engine coming their way, they ducked into the nearest alley, tucked in behind trash cans and piles of shipping boxes. *Survivors*, he thought? Until his ears adjusted, and he realized from what direction the sounds were coming.

The car was sleek and black, the men within dressed in matching black uniforms, their faces covered with German gas masks. They looked like predatory insects, man-sized ants, preparing to eat the remains of civilization.

The car stopped practically across the street from them. The forward passenger door opened, letting a lanky, tall figure exit the vehicle. Leaning against the opened door, he first removed his right glove. Reaching into an inner pocket of the black-on-black uniform, he removed a pack of cigarettes, tapping one out against the knuckles of his other hand. With the back of the still-gloved hand, he pushed up the gas mask, revealing a young face, before he perched the cigarette in the corner of a thin-lipped mouth.

"Shouldn't do that," the driver cautioned him, the words muffled but understandable.

Sparking the cigarette with a trench lighter the likes of which the Ghoul had himself used half a world away, the smoker asked, "What?" He took the gas mask off completely, letting his sweat-damp, short blonde hair chill in the brisk night air. "Smoke?"

His accent was unmistakably European, but not strictly German. Austrian, maybe?

The driver exited the car, lifting his own mask as he beckoned across the hood of the car for a smoke of his own. He caught the pack tossed to him, tapped out his own cigarette, and lit up with a flip lighter that sparked to life with a sharp *zing!*

"Taking your mask off. The doctor will have your skin if you bring anything back with you."

The blonde shook his head, exhaling smoke. "Not likely. You heard the mad doctor: it disperses too quickly. Half an hour after it was let loose, it was useless."

The driver shook his head, looking out into the night. "What are we doing here?" he asked, and shook, with cold or revulsion, Ghoul couldn't tell.

Both rear doors of the car opened, a matched set of insect men getting out, guns at the ready.

"*Unternehmen! Siehst du das mädchen?*" one of them barked, followed by something that Ghoul couldn't quite catch, but the drift was there. Trouble coming.

Flicking away their unfinished cigarettes, the driver and blondie pulled down their masks, pulled pistols from shoulder holsters, and started looking around with increased haste. The driver and one of the back seat soldiers stalked over to the pile of bodies that Ghoul had left in front of the township building, examining the corpses from a distance, obviously reluctant to risk getting any closer.

Blondie and the other soldier trolled the street, shining flashlights down alleys and in windows. *They know I'm here.*

"There's no way they could have made it away from those things," the driver shouted across the street. "We'll probably find their bodies in the morning, underneath this pile of offal."

Blondie stopped before the alley in which Ghoul and the girl hid and shone his light down it fleetingly. It was obvious that he expected to find nothing. His companion was right, he was sure of it, but T's had to be crossed. With a sigh that could be heard a dozen feet away, he stopped his examination, and strolled back toward the car.

With a jolt, he stopped, aiming his flashlight and pistol off to his right, firing off three shots before the others had time to react. A dozen or more of the infected were upon them all at once, drawn no doubt by the sound of the car. Like a great, bloody smear, one of the soldiers was gone, dead before he'd even had time to scream. The driver followed, plowed under the wave of corrupted humanity.

Blondie had just made it to the car when his feet were taken out from under him. Shrieking like a madman, he rolled onto his back and began firing anywhere and everywhere in a futile attempt to get away from his attackers. He did manage to wing a few before his arm was thrown wide. The more shots followed: the first into the fleeing back of his final companion, who'd nearly made it to the safety of car. His body crumpled like wet newspaper, his spine obviously severed, which might have been a blessing, given what the horde did to him once he was down. The second shot went into blondie himself, as the arm was twisted around unnaturally, the elbow dislocated, the bullet taking him in the throat. Whether he bled out before the monsters ripped him apart the Ghoul never knew, as his blasted form was mercifully covered from view by his killers.

Silently, Ghoul moved backward down the alley, further into deep shadow, urging the girl along. If she made a noise now they'd both be done for. He hoped to God that she was too terrified to make a peep.

Rounding the back of the buildings, he was amazed to see how well she was holding up. She was obviously terrified, as was he, but her face was set and determined under her wide eyes. There was sternness to her that he admired, but that also confused him. Mouse, indeed.

◉◉◉

They could still hear the sounds of the beasts in the street attacking what was left of the four Germans. Even for someone who'd lived the kind of life he'd lived, it was vile. Like the score to a painting by Bosch.

Still keeping to the shadows, they continued onward towards the castle. Even from a distance, he could make out its shining windows, the wrought iron fence that surrounded it, easily standing twelve feet high. If the detritus of humanity that infested this place was attracted to lights, sounds, then surely they would be clustered around the castle. But how many were there?

"How many people lived here before this mess?" he asked. They'd made it to the end of the street, and all that was before them now was miles of open land and trees before their final destination.

"Dunno," she answered, following in his footsteps. "Couple dozen families all told, lots of kids to each, plus grandkids or great grandkids for some of the older folks. I had to guess, I'd say a few hundred, maybe as much as three."

He stopped dead for a minute and shook his head. His breath caught for a moment. It was a humbling experience, to feel unsuited to a task. Then he set his jaw. It didn't matter. Some things, there's no way to be up for them. No way for anyone to pull them off. Didn't mean you didn't try.

But they'd never get in on foot. They'd either get caught out in the open stretch by some corrupted citizen out for a stroll, or else they'd get to the gates surrounding the castle and get turned into so much gristle when the cluster of corrupted people ground them to a halt there. With reluctance, he turned back toward where they'd just come from.

They'd need a car...

"Stay here," he whispered. "Don't be seen, don't be heard, and when you see me coming, be ready to go."

She reached out once, as if to stop him from leaving her alone, but stopped herself and nodded acceptance. By the time he'd reentered the alley, she was nowhere to be seen.

With each step back up the alley, his feet grew heavier, the air thicker, his senses sharper. His heart beat like a drum section in his ears, and an irrational part of him felt that everyone within miles must have heard it. He pulled the scarf back over his mouth to hide some of his exhalations again.

Slim automatic in one hand, he stopped behind the same trash bin that he'd been hiding behind minutes earlier. Viewing the scene, he saw that the four Germans were nowhere to be seen, only bloody smears left behind to signify their passing. The corrupted were also not in evidence, though he could hear them moving around not too far off. Looking at the car, he could hear the engine muttering. The first good news he'd had in hours.

Steeling himself, he crept to the edge of the alley, tentatively peeking around a corner to see where his attackers were. He saw them, no more than twenty feet away, milling around, looking for someone to infect. He pitied them as much as they sickened him.

With a bracing breath, he lunged for the car, making the open passenger door before the first of the corrupted noticed him. Sliding across the seat, he shifted into gear and floored it, rounding buildings and crashing through side streets, drawing the horde away from where he'd left the girl. Wind stung his eyes, three of the car's doors still open as their occupants had perished before having the opportunity to close them, the last only shut because of a trash can that he'd smashed into in his mad haste to be away.

Screeching up behind the buildings, he saw the girl leave her hiding spot, rushing to meet him. She'd no sooner slid into the passenger side, slamming the door behind her, when she looked over her shoulder and shrieked.

Pulling himself up from the bloody clutter of the back seat was one of the sad citizens of Quinnstown, eyes rolling back in his head, teeth exposed and reaching.

Marlene pushed herself backward onto the dash, kicking at the poor creature as it tried to get a lock on her. Terrified she might be, but hardly useless: she aimed the revolver that Ghoul had given her in Wolfe's office, and fired five shots at the intruder. Three struck him in the chest; the final two in the face, relieving him of the back of his head, and the exiting bullets relieving the car of its back window.

Ears ringing at the five loud explosions in such close confines, Ghoul drug the girl down from the dash. "Nice shooting," he groaned, wincing.

◉◉◉

Peddle to the floor, they sped across the practically empty distance between the town and the sinister castle. The road leading there was rutted at best, an old wagon trail that would have broken a wooden wheel in minutes, and played hob with the shocks of the streaking black car. If they made it there without a blowout, he'd be amazed.

"What are you planning to do?" Marlene asked, head bouncing off the roof as they hit another deep pothole.

"I'm hoping," he told her, swerving to avoid a particularly big hole that would have bottomed them out for sure, "that the folks at the gate will see a familiar car and open up before they realize we're not their *liebe, alte freunde.*"

"And once we're inside the gate?" she asked.

He looked at her from the corner of his eye, still avoiding bad slices of road and an increasing number of trees. After a breath, he replied, more to himself than his companion, "Kill my way to the truth, I figure."

They turned past a tree, and saw the first of the infected inhabitants of

She looked over her shoulder and shrieked.

the town. With no chance to avoid the stumbling, gyrating woman, they plowed head-on into her. One of the headlights exploded with the impact. The woman was hurled onto the hood of the car, where she met the windshield with a savage impact.

Glass spiderwebbed, and those parts of her head and body not damaged horribly by the collision, forced their way through the glass. Bleeding more than should have been possible for a living thing, she forced an obviously shattered arm through a growing hole in the glass, fingers that were bent in all manner of unnatural directions grasping at the occupants of the car.

With no hesitation, Ghoul again drew his pistol and relieved the woman of her suffering with a perfectly placed round to the head. Her arm flopped, dead, while her poor head hung there, trapped in the confines of the spiderwebs.

Trying to see around the dead obstacle, he did his best to avoid the increasing number of beasts stumbling in front of them, each too decimated mentally from this terrible disease that they'd been assaulted with to know to move out of the way. They saw victims, someone to infect, and they would risk anything to get at them.

Three more times he hit people, never purposefully, the final one rolling under the car, something on him jagged enough to pop one of the front tires, hardly more than a dozen feet from the surrounding gate of the horrible castle.

The gate was easily eighteen feet high, welded iron, as thick as a man's leg. Each rail was barbed at the top, to prevent anyone, or anything, from going over it. Before it were easily seventy five unfortunate victims of tonight's events.

The central entry was guarded by a dozen men, each dressed as blondie and his companions had been: Black on black suits, German gas masks, with added wood-stocked rifles. Kar 98's. Germans...they stood half a dozen feet back from the gate, out of reach of prospective invaders, but close enough to shoot if they had to.

When the guards saw the car coming, they scrambled into action. Firing in four man rotations, they cleared the immediate entry to the castle grounds, enough so that the gate could be partially opened, just far enough for the car to charge inside. They continued firing until the gate was again closed, not a single invader having made it past them.

The car rounded a circular driveway that fronted the castle with sparks being thrown from the rim of the popped tire as it ground its way along gray stone, leaving a pair of deep divots in the ground behind it. As they ground on, Ghoul took a moment to take in their surroundings: The grounds were easily a hundred yards square, the castle off-center and toward the front. Behind it, hardly visible from that angle, was a small air strip, a two-seat crop duster parked there. Beyond that, seemingly endless, well-maintained grounds, until you met the other side of the encircling gate.

Reaching for the door handle, Ghoul was stopped dead when he felt the barrel of a pistol pressed against the back of his head. In spite of himself, he smirked; he'd known it.

Her own revolver was empty; he'd counted the shots as she'd emptied it into the body in the back seat. Taking account of himself, he noticed the lack of weight under his right arm. With his adrenalin pumping, he'd hardly noticed when she'd lifted his pistol.

"Please take the other one from your left side," she instructed him. Pressing the barrel more harshly against his head she added, "Slowly."

He did as she instructed, handing the second weapon through the opened door to a black-clad bug soldier. Looking over his shoulder, he asked, "Anything else, fraulein?"

She smiled at him, and the look was predatory on her. "What makes you think I'm German?" she asked.

He smiled back. "I've exterminated my share of krauts."

The words had no sooner left Ghoul than the soldier behind him brought down the stock of his rifle, sending him off into an exhausted darkness that he wasn't sure he'd ever wake from.

◎◎◎

Ghoul was hardly conscious when he became aware of being dragged down the long hallway toward some ungodly oblivion. Head throbbing, he cracked his eyes to get a look around.

A pair of bug soldiers had him under the arms, dragging his along. He was a big enough fellow that each had to use both arms to haul him. In a pinch, he was fairly sure he could handle them. He strained his ears, trying to get an idea of how many might be following. He could just make out two other distinct sets of footfalls. Each belonging undoubtedly to a man with a gun at the ready. This could get hairy.

He was indoors, he could tell that. The sounds of the corrupted citizens were evident, but distant, separated from him by one wall at least. To his left was moonlight, filtered through thick glass. The castle was large, but nowhere near big enough to take a long while to get him to wherever they were taking him. He'd only been out for a brief moment, then. But why hadn't they just killed him? The girl? Was Marlene Moore, or whatever her real name was, keeping him around for amusement? Whoever she was, it was obvious that she enjoyed desperate thrills. Otherwise, why be outside the gate at all, in the nightmare that surrounded it?

Somewhere along the long hallway, they stopped dragging him, and while his two crutches continued to hold him up, one of the men behind moved forward to open a locked door. When the door was open, he acted.

With a vicious kick, Ghoul sent the man with the key into the side of the door, his foot planted on the guards neck, breaking it against the door itself. Quick hands grabbed his crutches by their heads, smashing them together with enough force to shatter the lenses of their gas masks, dropping them to the floor unconscious.

When he heard the commotion behind him of the last man shouldering his weapon, Ghoul figured he was done for. The hit to his head earlier had slowed him, and his reflexes weren't up to snuff. He'd die here, in a hallway, the smallest battlefield he'd been on, with nothing to show for it.

But suddenly she was there. Kneeling on the floor just outside the door, one of the fallen soldier's guns in her hands, aimed up at the last guard standing, was Marion McGivern. Her scarlet hair was a matted mess, and she was bruised all over. Whoever had worked her over had done a job, but she'd had worse. In the more than a decade he'd known her, he'd seen her stand up to the abuses of monsters, up to and including the one that'd cost her an eye. What she'd done to get her own back against the man who took it was something Ghoul would never forget.

"*Lass es fallen, Fritz, oder ich lüfte dich,*" she told the guard.

For maybe a heartbeat the guard considered. Then with slow motions he upended the gun and handed it over to Ghoul. Marion's keen eye on him afterword, the guard hauled his companions into the vacated cell that had contained the diminutive redhead, lastly dragging in the corpse. Carefully stripping each of them of their weapons—spare ammunition for the rifles, knives, one of Ghoul's own pistols with accompanying magazines, the other undoubtedly still held by Marlene Moore as some kind of demented trophy—he piled the lot outside the door and backed into the cell.

"*Knien,*" she said, following him in. *Kneel.* With reluctance, he did so, his back to her, undoubtedly waiting for a shot that would snuff his light for good. With a force surprising in someone of such small stature, she brought the rifle down on the back of his head, knocking him unconscious, but not killing him.

Locking the door and dropping the keys into a large potted plant a little way up the hallway, she turned to look at her friend, and asked, "What took you so long?"

◎◎◎

"Did you bring the twins?" she asked as they rushed back toward the gate.

"Which ones?" he asked. Within the small confines of their little group of trouble-sorters, there were two sets of twins: A very smart, if somewhat odd, brother and sister called Think and Thunk; and a frighteningly effective pair of wetworks siblings: The brother, Aym, easily the best shot Ghoul had ever known, and the sister, Act, the most dangerous hand-to-hand fighter he'd ever seen.

"Right now, either would do," Marion answered. At the large double door that led outside to the courtyard, she peeked through the side windows, looking for trouble. Perhaps forty yards away, she saw the few remaining guards, taking the occasional shot at the invading citizenry. The citizenry, for their part, would back away for short whiles, then charge the gate again, endlessly attempting to overwhelm the men stationed there.

"We need to open the gate," she said.

"All right, and why?" he asked.

She sighed. "There's at least eight folks out there, and once the shooting starts, they'll come running."

"If they can hear it out here, through walls, over the sounds of their own shots."

Without looking at him, she asked, "Are you willing to take that chance?"

He thought for a moment, and shook his head. The guards at the gate might get dropped by the invaders easily enough, but they might stand their ground, keeping both busy while Ghoul and Marion did what needed doing.

"How's the gate open?" he asked. "I was busy when we arrived."

"Electric lock," she said. "Control's over there." She pointed. Ten feet inside the gate, guarded by a single man, his back to them. In a sea of activity, he was an island of calm, looking at his companions as they kept close watch on the invaders, but far enough from them to not be endangered. "I can get him."

Ghoul looked through the window at the men guarding the gate. Their complete focus was on the other side. As far as they knew they were safe here. They'd probably never see her coming.

"Think anyone else is rounding the grounds?" he asked.

"Doubt it," she replied. "Probably why they have these guys right out front: keeps the unsavory types out, but also gives them a focus, draws them to this one spot. Cute, as long as it works."

They stood there in near perfect silence for another moment before he nodded.

"Do what you do," he told her.

Silently, she exited the castle, leaving her pilfered rifle with Ghoul, unsheathing an equally pilfered knife that she'd taken from one of the unconscious or dead guards inside. Like a shadow, she crept up behind the target, while her friend stayed in the house, her gun in his arms, sighting in on every guard in turn, ready to eliminate anyone that might see her coming. He needn't have worried.

With a quick slice, she'd opened the neck of her man, and wrung the electric lever that controlled the gate, jamming the knife into the control to jam it. The panic, when it happened, was complete and sudden.

When the gate began opening, the guards jolted, shouting and aiming their guns in panic. They'd been incredibly professional earlier when he'd come driving through, but they'd had some notice then. Now it was all a cluster show, and they were losing their minds. Each turned to see why their fellow had opened the gate and saw the small redhead running, but none could bother to take a shot at her, as things were instantly life and death for them.

Charging through the large double doors again, Ghoul slamming them behind her and pushing nearby furniture in front of them, she stood panting. Outside, the barrage of gunfire was epic. There was no formation to it, no discipline. It was every man for himself and in time none of them would be left.

Taking the Rifle back, she gasped, "Come on. Let's go kill him."

◎◎◎

The castle was oddly laid out, to say the least. With the exception of thin rooms, like the one in which Marion had been imprisoned (and which was currently occupied by three unconscious guards, and one corpse), the outer layer of the building seemed to be a shell for a more or less hollow interior: a facade, but for which circle of hell?

"What kind of numbers are we looking at?" he asked her as they rounded another corner, looking for entry to the inner recesses of the building.

"He must want to keep his operations small. Never saw more than a dozen and a half, all told, including the guards, our old pal the Butcher, and that cow of his," she said, grinding her teeth at this last.

"What's the skinny on that, anyway?" he asked, smirking.

Marion grunted. "God only knows. Niece, daughter, mutant love child. Whatever the case, she needs to be put to sleep before we finish up here."

Hearing the chill in her voice, Ghoul asked, "Do I even want to know what she did?"

"Nope," she answered. "But she won't be doing it again."

A few dozen yards from where they'd started, they finally found a door leading into the bowels of the building. He'd half expected it to be a massive, steel thing, with lockworks out of a bank, but what they found was a simple wooden door, adorned with not a single lock, but rather a basic knob, like the one on his bathroom at home.

Their eyes met, and she shrugged. What the hey, they were already there.

Slowly turning the knob, he opened the door on silent, well-oiled hinges and slid in, crouching. Closing it softly behind them, they took in their surroundings. The upper recesses of the large room were mostly dark, the majority of the light being reserved for the floor. Encircling the walls were landings and stairways, each red carpeted and dark stained wood. They led down three stories, to a large circular floor, on the center of which was the main attraction.

Four people were down there, each in the matching gas masks that Ghoul had gotten used to. Two were in neck to ankle white lab coats, with matching white leather boots. One was slim and feminine, blonde hair shooting helter-skelter around the straps that held the mask in place. It was the last who truly drew the eye, however.

"Your games will be the death of you!" he shouted at Marlene Moore. Napoleon Chort. Appolyhon. Dioval. Teufel. The Butcher.

He was taller than Ghoul remembered. Perhaps a touch over six feet. His body was thin, old man thin, and nearly hairless; what hair there was thin, wiry, and snow white. The exposed skin of his arms, shoulders, neck were a patchwork of thin scars, like he wasn't in fact a man, but a modern day Frankenstein's monster. He wore a white butcher's apron, tied loosely around his thin waist. Similarly colored rubber gloves adorned his arms, as high up as his pointy elbows. His trousers were the same snow white as his hair, fading effortlessly into his white leather boots.

Ghoul's teeth ground together.

"Then you'd just have to make me again, dear," Marlene replied gleefully. She danced around the room while she talked, like a child on a playground, rather than an adult in an abattoir of horror. "Someone had to collect those awful papers that Wolfe had collected on you."

In the center of the room, easily twenty feet across and a story and a half tall, was a circular cage. Within it, elevated by cables bound to his waist, ankles, and wrists was a single man, his body in wretched convulsions, flailing and screaming soundlessly. A tight canvas muzzle held his jaws closed, and muffled any sounds he might have made. Even from a distance it was obvious he didn't have much life left in him.

Circling the room were tables clustered with scientific apparatus the use for which Ghoul couldn't even guess. Interspersed between these tables were others, decorated with more terrible things: underlit glass display cylinders, filled with green and orange liquids, body parts of seemingly endless variety floating within.

To one side of the central cage, on an elevated stage, was an operating table, upon which was secured a still living, though hardly, young man, and at which The Butcher stood, a pair of scalpels in his hands. While he talked, The Butcher cut into the young man, removing the horrible treasures that his body hid.

"How many times must I remake you?" The Butcher asked, lifting up an organ, and examining it closely, while his victim twitched one last time and died, unnoticed. "What has it been now? Three times?"

"Four," she danced. "You always forget St. Petersburg."

He stopped his work for a moment and stood still, concentrating. "Of course," he said at last. "How could I forget St. Petersburg?"

"Bah!" she shouted, twirling like a ballerina. "And why should I worry about such mortal things? Thanks to your masters, and your own necromancy, I never need to fear actual death. So, I ask you: why not have as much fun as I can?"

He put his scalpels down and turned to face her, a large insect, covered in the blood and viscera of his victim. "I think sometimes that your constant brushes with oblivion have left you unhinged. Perhaps growing you anew from the remains of your mind has left you with an addiction to death. A fetish that no amount of living can undo."

With a shrug, he turned back to the table. However, before he could continue his work the air at the top of the room exploded to life with green and gray light, small motes of illumination swirling and twisting until they drew together to form an inhuman face, easily ten feet tall, floating in the air.

Looking up at the gray-green face, with more annoyance than awe, The Butcher bemoaned, "How nice of you to drop by. To what do I owe the pleasure?"

The face was shaped like an upside down egg, bulbous at the top, and hairless, with a practically nonexistent jaw and chin. Its eyes were too big, almond-shaped, and black. Its mouth was a thin slit, too low in the face. There was no nose, but rather a pair of small gashes where the nostrils might have been. It was horrible and inhuman, and entirely beyond the experiences of either Marion or Ghoul. Yet, somehow, in some deep part of their subconscious, they both felt that they recognized it, feared it, hated it…

"It has come to our notice that we should keep a closer watch on your activities," it replied, its voice booming. "You, and those like you, tend to be pulled off into other projects, if left to your own devices."

"Come now," The Butcher said, "Things have gone exceedingly well here with this little Armageddon of yours. Everyone is dead or dying, it spreads like no plague ever. The people of this country will be broken in mind and spirit in days. And for what it's worth, make no mistake: there are no others like me. I am a singular horror the likes of which mankind has never seen."

The face looked hard at The Butcher. It said, "We are aware of your love for your accomplishments. Do not let your ego get in the way of progress. We are not a forgiving people."

As quickly as it had appeared, the face vanished. It took a few moments for Ghoul's and Marion's eyes to readjust to the fresh darkness. By the time they did, The Butcher was looking solidly at them, his body relaxed.

A smile in his voice, he shouted, "Why don't you join us?"

◉◉◉

Reluctantly they stood. The Butcher looked at them, his bearing amused. Marlene Moore twirled off to his left, Ghoul's pilfered pistol in her hand. The other two men—scientists? Doctors?—were apparently dumbfounded by the unexpected interruption.

"What was that?" Ghoul asked, waving a hand in the general direction of the vanished face of light.

The Butcher shrugged. "My masters," he answered. "Or so they think. I'm not completely sure, honestly. It's possible they're travelers in time, come back to help me help them take over the world. They could be life-forms from other worlds, or dimensions, branching out from their own

The Butcher looked at them, his bearing amused.

homes in the hopes of creating a subject race here. They've been less than forthcoming with the details. Yet, they're very direct about what they expect me to do here.

"We each have our parts to play in rewriting the world, you see. The Bolsheviks in Russia, the madman who gained control of Germany a few months back, even our own homegrown Communists and fascists. We're all doing our part to remake the world in their image. So many places are easy to control. Make their hearts bleed and they'll give you anything. Guilt is always a great motivator.

"You Americans are always a problem. You have no heart to trick. The needs of the masses will never convince you people to give up their precious freedoms. They would go to the gallows or the guillotine rather than bend the knee. Them you have to break, and nothing breaks the spirit of the American like fear. Fear of sickness, fear of death. Once my beautiful disease is unleashed on the world at large, they won't even think to fight us. They'll put the collars on themselves, and thank us for the boot we plant on their necks!"

He stopped his monologue suddenly, and pointed a bloody, gloved hand at his visitors. The Butcher said, "I remember you. Both of you. You, woman, were in Germany near the end of the last war. I recall you on the arm of some self-important man or another. Far too attractive to be with someone like him, I believed. Were they all not fools, I'd have told them you were a spy. As it was, I had no more loyalty for the Germans then than I have for their Fuhrer now."

They descended the stairs, Ghoul in front of Marion. He wasn't being chivalrous: she was a better shot, and if he could buy her a few moments by working as a shield, then so be it.

"And you," The Butcher's voice grinded down into a low growl. "I remember you. You nearly killed me last time, you know that? I bet you figure you missed with that shot; that I got away because of your own clumsiness. But you were wrong."

With a thin hand, he lifted up his mask, showing a face horribly scarred, patchwork skin hardly covering a face too thin by far. The lips on the right ride of that face pulled back tightly, showing false teeth that scowled regardless of expression. The eye on that side sat crookedly in a socket mismatched with its opposite. On the left side was a small, puckered scar: the entry wound, from the shot that had blown out the other half of the monster's face. A shot taken by Ghoul more than a decade earlier; one that should by rights have snuffed this miserable, foul creature.

"You didn't miss me, my old friend," the fiend continued, pulling the mask back down. By then his guests had reached the floor, and were circling the room, each heading in the opposite direction.

"How are you still kicking?" Ghoul asked. In spite of himself, he felt a need to know, before he finished the job this time.

The Butcher nodded. "Fair enough. Do you know how old I am? I've seen two centuries pass over, whether you believe it or not. Not through magic or alchemy, as my dear wife insinuates." He gestured toward the mad, dancing Marlene Moore. She and Marion moved ever closer to each other, both armed, both waiting.

"Science!" The Butcher shouted. "For decades, I'd been experimenting with a great many things, in an attempt to prolong my life. I'd succeeded already in creating a number of new bodies for my dearest, there. But I couldn't risk doing such to myself. Much as I still love the murdering little minx, I fear that my dear wife has been driven quite mad by the strains of constant death and rebirth."

At her mention, Marlene stopped her insane dancing, to look disapprovingly at her husband. "Now, pooh!" she admonished, pouting.

"I still love you, my dear," The Butcher explained. "But there is simply no denying it: you're quite cracked." As if accepting her husband's condemnation, she shrugged her shoulders and started spinning again.

For a moment longer than necessary, Ghoul followed her with his eyes. In that single moment, The Butcher, with speed and strength that should have been beyond someone his age and size, was on Ghoul, one bloody gloved hand holding onto Ghoul's wrist, keeping the pistol pointed away from them, the other with a vice-grip upon his enemy's throat, lifting him into the air like a doll. The Butcher leaned in close to his quarry.

"I've experimented for decades, you know. Lifetimes. I'd managed to instill myself with chemicals and machinery that made astounding changes to my body." With a squeeze of his hand, the madman began to crush Ghoul's clenched wrist. This was no man. Beneath the skin and muscle, Ghoul could feel hard steel, rather than bone. "My head no longer houses all of my mind. It's spread out all over my body, countless redundancies, each guaranteeing that no matter the damage that might befall my form, my mind will live on! Cellular consciousness! I'm the only one for the task I've set myself you see: there's no one else alive that might save humanity from itself!"

As The Butcher had made his mad grab for Ghoul, Marlene Moore had done much the same toward Marion McGivern, though with somewhat different results. With a particularly energetic spin, the mad woman had launched herself at the small redhead, with the intention of dropping her in her tracks. She hadn't counted on Marion's reflexes, however.

When she saw that her attacker was instantly too close to bring her rifle to bear in time, Marion had upended the stock of the weapon into the whirling knee cap of the other woman, shattering it with a sickening crack. Marlene had fallen to the ground, leg bent at an unnatural angle. Without making so much as a sound, she had tried to stand again, only to have the stock brought down a second time on the small of her back, with much the same result. Her legs useless, her prey having the upper hand, she did indeed scream now. Though it was not a scream of pain, but rather one of frustration, of impotence. It was the scream of a spoiled child, one who was never told "no," who suddenly didn't get her way.

Pity at last overtook the raging hate that Marion felt for this broken enemy. Or perhaps it simply accompanied it. Still looking into the shouting, animal face of this villain, she quickly shouldered the rifle, and with a carefully placed shot between the eyes, stopped the anger and frustration and pain, all at once.

Turning the rifle on the others, she saw Ghoul held in the air, his face turning red and purple, the skeletal form of The Butcher apparently unburdened by the big man that he was holding. The other two men rushed at her, whatever ramshackle instruments they could grab in hand. Two quick shots put both down, dead before they even hit the floor.

The next round she placed firmly in the neck of The Butcher, at enough of an angle that the exiting round would miss her friend completely. The old lunatic released Ghoul's neck to grab at his own, a gurgling shout escaping his lips. In the moment that he was free, Ghoul struck the madman with his free fist, knocking loose the gas mask, and causing his enemy to release his wrist. Shoving the freed gun against the exposed face of his enemy, Ghoul fired three quick shots. Inhuman or not, The Butcher still could not keep his feet with so much tissue damage. He dropped onto his back and writhed, blood spilling everywhere, his head a grizzly blossoming flower.

Quite suddenly they became aware of other sounds within the house: shattering glass, rupturing wood, overturned furniture. The infected had breached the building.

Ghoul looked down at the still moving purpose of their visit, and emptied the last few rounds from his pistol. Still the monster moved, but only his arms and above: one of the shots must have hit the spine and paralyzed him.

Grabbing her friend by the sleeve, Marion growled, "Leave him. In a few minutes he'll have lots of pleasant company. That'll be the end of him. We don't have to die here."

Reluctantly, he followed her, spending one last moment looking down at the broken beast.

◉◉◉

Ghoul and Marion McGivern had just made the top of a flight of stairs opposite the one they'd only recently descended, and were opening the matching door found there when the one they'd entered through burst open and an army of corrupted humanity charged in. Eyes wide with near panic, they pushed through the exit, and ran for all they were worth toward the rear of the building.

Changing magazines while he ran, Ghoul drew a bead and dropped any obstacle in their way. Many of the small town's former citizens were roaming the calmly lit hallways, meeting their merciful maker only split seconds after seeing their approaching prey. Only a single one of The Butcher's soldiers was found, cringing in a corner, rifle held across his cowering chest, mind broken, simply waiting for oblivion. They ran past him, leaving him to whatever horrible fate he'd earned.

Thankfully, the building was laid out very simply, with no labyrinth of passageways or doors to nowhere. Through the windows that they passed, they could clearly see the small landing strip and the plane there. Each sent up a silent prayer that the thing was fueled at least enough to get them away from this place.

When at last they'd made their way to a rear door and rushed out into the night, it was very obvious that the infected had overtaken the house. Windows burst from inside, and a few unlucky souls plummeted to their death falling from them only to stop suddenly on the stonework below.

Within seconds of their exit, Ghoul and Marion were followed from the house by easily a dozen pursuers. The wretched souls were wracked by painful movements, every twitch an unbelievable agony. No matter their condition before their infection, the disease had done terrible things to their bodies. No doubt they'd be gone for good within hours.

Leaping into the pilot's seat of the canary yellow biplane, Ghoul groaned, "Start start, start," and began to turn it over while Marion pulled the chocks and jumped into her own seat. When the propellers spun to life, he nearly gave a cheer. It was instantly cut short by a set of gnarled hands grabbing onto the sides of his cockpit.

When the plane began to roll, the hands fell away. Looking over his shoulder for only a moment, Ghoul's blood ran cold: They were following. Hot on his heels more than a dozen furious, twisted mockeries of humanity shambled, arms outstretched, teeth exposed. Over the roar of the engine he could hear no sounds coming from them, but the screams of pain and fury and frustration were plain enough on their faces. Their wide, bulging eyes were imploring, condemning.

Picking up speed, nearing the three-quarter mark of the runway, Ghoul began pulling back on the stick. With slow bumps, he lifted them off, missing the far end of the enclosing gate with the plane's wheels by perhaps a foot.

Once airborne, he checked the fuel gauge and was relieved to see a nearly full tank. Knowing that they had some cushion, he banked the plane, and circled the building. Below, he could see the victims of The Butcher roaming the grounds, and more windows being shattered as chairs and lamps and coat racks were thrown through them. In the eastern end of the building, he could faintly detect smoke and low, flickering lights. He couldn't be certain, but was fairly sure that a fire was somehow starting inside the building. The thought of this made him somehow happy.

Let it burn, he thought…

Leaving the airspace above the castle, he flew them out over the town, where not a sign of life showed. It was dead, a ghost town born of the evil machinations of a two-hundred-year-old monster.

◉◉◉

Crawling along the floor toward the body of his wife, The Butcher cursed the names of his attackers. He was hurt, no doubting that, but as the saying went, this wasn't his first rodeo. Though it might take him years, he would get himself together, reestablish the use of his legs, sew his head together.

He looked out of his one good eye, and found that even focusing that one was something of a strain. Loath as he was to admit it, his enemies had done a job on him. He doubted that he'd ever been this hurt in his long life. It was only due to his twisting of science that he was alive at all.

Reaching the body of his fallen beloved, he laid a tender hand upon her bloody cheek.

"Not to worry, my love," he told her. "I've made you back from less." His voice sounded odd to his ear, the words slurred and whistled. Softly touching, he probed his mouth with bony fingers, and felt a rent there at the top. The upper jaw wasn't quite whole. Just wonderful: another thing to fix.

For not the first time in his life, he was grateful for the chemical concoction that he'd stumbled upon decades earlier that gave him not only the ability to consciously remove any inconvenient pain he might be feeling, but which had also dispersed the atoms of his brain throughout his body. Any mere mortal would have instantly succumbed to his current injuries, as any would have after what Ghoul had done to him near the end of the last war. However, he was no mere mortal. He might never be a god, but his reign would nevertheless last forever.

Unaccountably, he suddenly found himself being pulled from the body of his lovely Marlene. Turning a blasted head to look behind himself, he felt absolute terror for the first time in his long, long life.

There were only a few of them, perhaps three or four. He couldn't actually tell: his single working eye wouldn't let him focus. As if looking through a fog, he saw them grabbing at him, pulling him apart, one bloody joint at a time. Their animal rage and fury gave them strength that their desiccated bodies should have denied them.

"No!" his hissing voice shouted, dimly seeing himself being dismantled by this rage mob that he'd created. By then his legs were gone, along with many of his endless redundancies of consciousness. His torso and arms followed. Lastly his already mostly obliterated head.

All the while, his cells, each with perfect, endless awareness of what was happening, shouted out in impotent fury at a torment that would go on simply forever…

◉◉◉

For the better part of an hour they flew, before spotting a small landing field close to Chester, Pennsylvania. Touching down more roughly than he'd intended, they were both nevertheless grateful to be on the ground again.

Engine shut, they sat for a few moments, enjoying the quiet.

Dawn was more than two hours away, but a light was on in the small post office at the side of the field. A door opened, and a tall, thin postman started his slow, ambling walk toward them.

"We need to call someone," Ghoul said. "Get that burg closed up tight, before someone gets out."

"Nothing to worry about, there," Marion told him, leaning her head back, eye closed. "That monster and his old lady did like to talk. When they caught me breaking into their place earlier tonight, I heard them saying about how this was all a test run. That the rabies strain that they made was so quick acting that it'd kill anybody got it in a couple hours. It's why they picked Quinnstown in the first place: too far from anywhere to have the subjects spread it out. They wanted to make sure all was good and ready before they dropped it in a city."

Ghoul shuddered, in spite of himself. A city, millions of people, reduced to vicious monsters. Unless things were handled quickly and right, they'd overtake the country in weeks. And that would be the end of the Great Experiment.

"How'd they get it into the people?" he asked. "Poison the water?"

She tapped the side of the plane. He looked down, and saw the canisters strapped to the side of the crop duster. They'd come in from the air, gassed the people with whatever vile concoction had been in those canisters, and flown on, leaving God only knew how many unsuspecting people to their horrible fate. His stomach felt queasy.

"Help you folks?" the postman asked, coming alongside the plane.

Ghoul jumped down from the plane and looked at the man. "You have a telephone, friend?" he asked. He'd been to Chester before, and though it wasn't exactly a societal hub, it was hardly rustic, either.

"Party line," the postman answered, throwing a thumb over his shoulder. "Welcome to use it, but might take a few to get the operator on the line. Means well, but she's slower'n hell."

Ghoul smiled, glad to be back in civilization.

"Might want to keep an eye on the plane, though," the postman added. "Couple kids 'round the way tried to go off on a joyride with the mail plane last week."

"Many thanks," Ghoul said. "My friend'll stay with the plane. How close are the police? We have a bit of a problem needs their attention."

The postman looked at the nearly sleeping Marion still sitting in the plane, and nodded. "Couple miles. We get 'em on the line, they should be here in five-ten minutes. Follow me, fellah."

It was nearly nightfall again by the time things were getting well on their way. The police had met them at the airfield, followed soon thereafter by representatives of the Army. The plane was cordoned off, the canisters retrieved by professionals. Less than an hour later, the town was surrounded, based on nothing more than the name and reputation of Ghoul in his professional guise as Lieutenant Marvin MacCormac.

When they at last moved in, the town was dead. What few citizens hadn't been killed by Ghoul or the gate guards at the castle were dead, killed by the virus that had corrupted them. As for the castle itself, it was nothing more than a raging blaze, smoke filling the air thick as butter. No one moved around without a gas mask firmly secured to their faces. Though there was little chance that the sickness bred in the lab could survive the blaze that now encompassed it, none felt that it was worth the risk of not taking precautions.

For better or worse, Quinnstown was gone, erased from the world like a sad, half-remembered nightmare.

◎◎◎

Stumbling into his small office/home the following night, exhausted from more than two days of constant movement and little rest, Ghoul dropped in a plush chair behind a battered desk and breathed a long-suppressed sigh of relief. Sleep nearly overtook him, before the phone on his desk rang.

Picking up the handset from its cradle, he asked, without opening his eyes, "What took you so long?"

"So what happened?" replied the voice of his mysterious benefactor. For years he'd been sending Ghoul and his companions on trips around the country, and occasionally around the world, with no mention of who he was, or what his final motivations might have been. He was a mystery, and Ghoul liked mysteries. Little did his benefactor realize that Ghoul had already cracked his.

"Another incursion. Had a run in with The Butcher of Berlin."

A gasp. Actual surprise? "Did you kill him?"

"I'd say he's dead, yes, but I didn't see it."

"What was he trying to do?"

For ten minutes or so Ghoul clued his caller in on the events of the past few days. In the end there were very few questions from the voice on the other side of the call. They'd been through this kind of thing before, though hardly anything quite as brutal as this. Ghoul couldn't help but worry that this might be the start of something worse than he was used to. That the world was going to get redder now.

"You did good," the voice said.

"We did good," Ghoul answered.

"How is Marion?"

"Sterner stuff was never made."

Ghoul could feel the nod over the line.

"Get some rest," his benefactor told him. "It'll start again soon. I need you ready. The world needs you ready."

"Yep," he answered, placing the handset back in its cradle. He put his feet up on the desk, and dropped into a deep, just sleep.

THE END

ABOUT THIS ONE

Much as I enjoy this story, and as fun as it was to write, even I've got to admit there's nothing terribly new or groundbreaking about it. In each and every sentence, I've let my inspirations hang on my sleeve. So what is there to say about it that doesn't sound perversely self-serving and arrogant? Let's see...

I've always loved The Spider. Which isn't to say that I don't like any of the other pulp giants: The Shadow, Doc Savage and crew, etc. But there's always been something about The Spider that grabbed me by the teeth and didn't let go. Maybe it was the perpetual feeling of an apocalypse held off by inches that permeates every word of Page's best Spider stories. Maybe it's that The Spider never toned down, but kept things hard as nails right up until the end. Or, being more realistic, maybe it's just that Page (the primary writer of the stories) was just such an incredible wordsmith. Regardless of character, or setting, or genre, the guy could knock it out of the park.

A couple of years ago I had an idea for a series of adventure stories starring a mysterious character called The Ghoul, who ran around a crumbling society in the slow process of falling apart, fighting to hold back the darkness for one more minute, hour, day. I might still use that, but honestly it went on the backburner because after my kids were born, I just couldn't handle the super grim any more. I can read it, and enjoy it, but as for writing it, my heart just isn't there. Too much of the optimist, I guess...

About a year ago, I saw a posting on the profile of Mr. Ron Fortier, calling all writers who might be interested in submitting to the new issue of Airship 27's Mystery Men (& Women). I was instantly intrigued, but more than that, I was inspired. The very basic idea of The Ghoul came back, though ground down to a more straightforward version, removing the crumbling society, embracing a pulp world, and dealing punishment to those as had it coming.

From the outset, I'd decided to emulate the Spider-esque presentation of maximum justice, not trying to tone down the character, but rather letting him and his companions be justice (or vengeance) incarnate. A less fascist, more covert Dredd, by way of Street and Smith.

Borrowing a version of my daughter, Eleanor's, Camera Woman (with her gracious permission, of course), I set into writing the thing. Though there were some fairly frustrating technical difficulties in the form of my laptop getting fried (though the info thereon was saved, thank God), the story progressed, a thousand words a day for the first five days, and the last 10,000 in a span of about 48 hours.

I'll tell you, this is just about the most fun I've ever had writing something. The story pulled itself forward, I was just along for the ride. Characters showed up that I didn't know were going to be there, and when the villain introduced himself, I was as shocked as anyone. Until he made his entry, all I had in my mind was a foggy vision of a mad scientist. When he dropped in, it was all him, and when he talked to his wife, I wasn't writing as much as transcribing. And don't even ask me where the floating light head came from. I know now who and what it is, but at the time, I was asking what the heck I was looking at.

I enjoyed visiting with Ghoul and Marion. I liked dropping casual mensions of their compatriots Think and Thunk, Aym and Act (both of whom are central to the current story that Eleanor and I are working on, following around Marion on New Year's Eve 1933), and dropping in a line from Ira Grimm, a reporter who starred in his own little adventure, "The Damnation Gate," a few years ago (available in the collection *The Judas Hymn*, he said, winking).

This world is building itself, and it's my job to chronicle it, for better or worse. So for as long as the adventures of this small cluster of violent avengers keep coming to me, I'm bound to scribble them down, and try to get you fine folks to read them. So, until next time, have a good one, and be good to one another.

◎◎◎

ELEANOR HAWKINS & HARDING McFANDDEN are a Pennsylvania-based daughter-father writing team. Kinda-sorta. "The Ghoul Strikes" is their first (published) collaboration, with many times many to come. They are currently at work on a solo Marion "Camera Girl" McGivern adventure that they hope will knock your socks off. All other things being equal, they just hope that you enjoy their story.

Like this book? Here's what's come before...

During the golden days of American pulps hundreds of masked avengers were created to battle evildoers around the globe. *The Black Bat, Moon Man, Domino Lady*, and the *Purple Scar* to name only a few of these amazing pulp heroes. Now in each all-new volume New Pulp writers introduce to pulp readers brand new pulp heroes cast in the mold of their 1930s counterparts.

In each volume of *Mystery Men & Women* find a collection brand new action-packed stories starring original heroes to thrill and excite pulp fans everywhere as brought to you by Airship 27 Productions.

Appearing For the First Time Anywhere!!
GRIDIRON by David Boop
and
Three more *brand new* pulp heroes!!

B.C. Bell • Thomas Deja
Joel Jenkins • C. William Russette

Gene Moyers • Thomas Deja
Michael Black & Ray Lovato

Teel James Glenn • Curtis Fernlund
Greg Hatcher & Dale Cozort

www.ingramcontent.com/pod-product-compliance
Lightning Source LLC
Chambersburg PA
CBHW051131260626
47170CB00005B/1769